THE MONKEY PUZZLE

The Monkey Puzzle

by

Mary Cummins

Dales Large Print Books
Long Preston, North Yorkshire,
BD23 4ND, England.

British Library Cataloguing in Publication Data.

Cummins, Mary
     The monkey puzzle.

     A catalogue record of this book is
     available from the British Library

     ISBN   1-84137-015-0 pbk

First published in Great Britain by Mills & Boon, 1970

Copyright ' 1970 by Mary Cummins

Cover illustration ' Viney by arrangement with P.W.A.
International Ltd.

The moral right of the author has been asserted

Published in Large Print 2000 by arrangement with William G.
Cummins

Dales Large Print is an imprint of Library Magna Books Ltd.

Printed and bound in Great Britain by
T.J. (International) Ltd., Cornwall, PL28 8RW

CHAPTER ONE

'That will do, Sarah. I will listen to no further excuses.'

Sarah Hudson bit her lip as she looked into Aunt Muriel's stern face, the tight lips betraying fierce anger, only controlled by great effort.

Muriel Duff looked older than her years. Her iron-grey hair was kept fiercely in control by rolling it into neat sausage curls, and two well-etched lines between nose and mouth gave her face a pinched look. She was very thin and rather angular, and Sarah often looked at the family album to reassure herself that Aunt Muriel had once been young and pretty.

But now she was furious, and Sarah had to keep a tight control on herself to face this anger.

'Only by the Grace of God are you not in prison with that revolting young man...'

'He isn't revolting!'

'Be quiet, Sarah! If he is charming, then he allows none of it to show on the surface. I told you three months ago that he was no companion for a young girl like you, and that his ideas were ill-conceived and born of ignorance and sheer laziness over taking the trouble to find out all his facts.'

'We were only on a protest march,' cried Sarah. 'For heaven's sake, Aunt Muriel, I...'

'A protest march! Against what? Against authority? ... the establishment? ... call it what you will. But what have you got to take its place? Clifford Ainslie has nothing. He just protests about everything which doesn't happen to suit him without a single idea in his head as to how to put it right.'

Muriel Duff's voice softened a little.

'You can't change the world overnight, my dear,' she said, looking at the young girl in front of her, whose pretty rounded cheeks were bursting with colour. 'It *is* changing. Values are vastly different even from my day, but it has to be done gradually, not by going out and getting yourself soaking wet, carrying a banner, while your abominable young man goes and hits a policeman and lands in jail.'

'At least we draw attention to the fact that things *are* wrong, and do need to be put right,' flashed Sarah.

'Perhaps,' her aunt conceded. 'Perhaps ... but don't go tearing down old beliefs until you've got better ones to put in their place.'

Muriel Duff sat back and looked at her niece. Sarah was nineteen, an elf of a girl with soft curly dark hair, large brown eyes and a small delicately-boned body. Her mother had been Muriel's younger sister, and the girl had been left in her care three years ago when Alice died. Howard Hudson had been killed in a plane crash when Sarah was only four.

Perhaps it was because she had only ever had women running her life that she had become infatuated with Clifford Ainslie as soon as she left school and went on to the College of Art and Design.

Though Sarah seemed to have spent more time sitting about in cafés with groups of long-haired students than getting on with her work. Muriel's lips had tightened once before when she had read a report of her work, and she had threatened then to withdraw her support if Sarah didn't pull up her socks.

But it seemed that her warning had fallen on deaf ears. Muriel, even after several long discussions, had never really been quite clear about the reason for so many student protests at the local College of Art. As far as she could see, excellent tuition was offered, the student helped financially by Government grant, and excellent prospects were available to the talented artist, designer or photographer. Sarah had chosen to be a designer of boxes for packaging, but so far she hadn't proved herself to be unusually gifted in that direction.

'I've had a talk with Mr Hilden, your Principal,' said Aunt Muriel, leaning back in her chair. 'Quite frankly, he's rather fed up with you, Sarah, and I don't blame him.'

Sarah pouted. If she looked at herself honestly, she knew she wouldn't blame Mr Hilden either. At first she had honestly tried to work, and seemed to have done quite well in her Foundation Course, but then she had got in with Clifford and the rest of the gang, and had learned that it was square just to work away, meekly, putting up with irritations which hadn't really worried her till then.

Clifford had opened her eyes. She could see all sorts of things to which she had been blind before, and she had unhesitatingly accepted his point of view over everything. Of course, it was silly to accept things just because they'd always been done that way. She had tried to explain that to Aunt Muriel time and time again, but when she tried to give examples, then she always forgot what they were when she hadn't Clifford around to make it all clear to her.

'Maybe I'm a nitwit,' she thought despondently. She had never really been all that clever, she decided, thinking back over the past few years.

'Mr Hilden wonders if you've got any alternative in mind for your future,' Aunt Muriel went on. 'He thinks that if you continue with design, unless you're really dedicated, then it will be a waste of time on your part, and on his trying to cope with you. And he doesn't think you're really dedicated. What do you say to that?'

Sarah bit her lip, her lashes fanning her cheeks. So she was being thrown out! She wouldn't see Clifford so often if she left. But maybe Clifford too … maybe Mr Hilden would throw him out, too…

Sarah's eyes were wide. Could Mr Hilden really do that to them?

'Is he really throwing us out?' she asked, and bit her lip a little.

'Yes, he really is,' Aunt Muriel told her. 'I knew you'd never really believed that,

Sarah, but you *were* warned.'

'I know,' said Sarah.

'So I think you ought to go away from here for a while, and quite frankly, I think it's time you learned to stand on your own two feet. Alice wouldn't thank me for spoiling you. Nor would Howard. You had parents to be proud of, and it's up to me to encourage you to be a girl who would be a credit to them. I tried that by trying to make the most of your talents through education. But now I'm going to make you stand on your own feet, and I suggest that you take a job I've heard about for you. That is, if you're offered the job. It's near Kendal in Westmorland.'

'Kendal! But that's miles away.'

'I know, my dear.'

Again Aunt Muriel's voice softened, then her mouth firmed again. She had been much too soft with Sarah, trying to make up to her for the loss of her parents. She had leaned over backwards to try to give the girl a good chance in life, but Sarah hadn't been

15

able to understand that she herself must grasp her opportunities. Sarah had been spoilt, she decided, regretfully, first by Alice, then by herself. Now she was going to throw Sarah to the wolves, and it would be up to her, then, to show what she was made of.

'What kind of job?' Sarah was asking.

Aunt Muriel sighed, then moved a few papers on her desk. She was a solicitor, and tended to bring quite a lot of her work home with her. Now the desk was busy with papers, but after a moment she found what she was looking for, a letter written on expensive blue-grey paper.

'I got a letter today from Constance Demaine. You remember my friend Mrs Demaine?'

Sarah wriggled uncomfortably in her seat.

'Vaguely,' she admitted. 'I remember her staying here once when I came with Mummy.'

'We were friends at school,' Aunt Muriel explained. 'Your mother knew Constance well, though she was too young to be close friends with her. Constance and I are the same age.'

Sarah nodded, waiting and fidgeting a little. She wondered what all this had to do with her future.

'The Demaines have a fine old house about two or three miles from Kendal. John was a landscape architect, but I don't think he was a good earner. At least, Constance never seemed to be very well off, even during his lifetime, though Simon got a good education...'

Aunt Muriel stopped suddenly, and frowned as she read the letter.

'I don't know what he did with it,' she admitted, 'though perhaps he has followed his father. He seems bent on an unusual venture, some sort of gardening centre. He probably trained in horticulture. At any rate, rather than give up the house which is really too big for them ... I've stayed there! ... Simon has laid out the grounds into a series of small gardens and he aims to sell these in some sort of way. People are invited to view them, and choose a design. It's a sort of garden shop, I suppose.'

Again Aunt Muriel frowned, but Sarah's interest was caught.

'That sounds brillers,' she said.

'Sarah, I don't like slang. Hm ... yes, it does sound quite a good idea. At any rate, they're employing more staff, and need a girl, no doubt to help keep books and things ... office work ... someone to help Constance, maybe. At any rate, she laments that she hasn't been able to find anyone suitable yet, and I wrote and asked her if she thought you might do.'

'Aunt Sarah! I know *nothing* about office work.'

'You can answer the phone, can't you? And write down messages. I gather they aren't specifying a girl with nine O levels and three As.'

Aunt Muriel's voice was dry, and Sarah flushed uncomfortably.

'Constance says they'll give you a try, and you can go and stay next week. She suggests you travel on Monday rather than Sunday. The train service may be poor, and Monday is a quiet day at the Centre. Simon will meet you at the station. So what do you say, Sarah?'

'Have I any choice?'

Aunt Muriel's lips tightened again.

'Only the obvious one. You're over eighteen, and now you're considered an adult, though I never approved of the age of discretion being eighteen and not twenty-one. Especially if I may say so, Sarah, with a young girl of nineteen in my charge.'

Sarah's eyes grew stormy.

'That's just the sort of narrow-minded attitude that Clifford and I protested about,' she cried.

'And a lot of good it did either of you. If you want to prove your maturity, then I suggest that you take this job Constance has offered you. Maybe you could get a better one for yourself, but I think you ought to get away from my protection for a while and learn to think for yourself. I may have done too much of that thinking for you, and Mrs Nesbit, our daily, has certainly looked after you more than was good for you.'

'I can do things for myself,' said Sarah proudly, her chin in the air.

'I'm sure you can,' agreed Aunt Muriel smoothly, 'but I'd feel much happier about you if you were still under some sort of protection, and I know Constance will provide that. It's rather a hard, cruel world, my dear, for those who have suddenly no one but themselves to lean on. I don't feel you're ready for that.'

Sarah said nothing. She had the utmost confidence in her own ability to look after herself, but there was no use arguing with Aunt Muriel.

Theirs had been a curious relationship. They loved each other, she was sure of that, but in an oddly detached sort of way. Aunt Muriel was very self-contained, and beyond an occasional peck on the cheek, she had never shown any strong affection for her niece.

At first Sarah had missed the warmth of her mother's love, but gradually she had come to accept the security Aunt Muriel had offered. It was a security of a warm, pleasant home, regular meals, Mrs Nesbit to look after her, and keep her bedroom tidy and her clothes neat, and just enough regular pocket money to be comfortable. Sarah had learned to take it all for granted, and had seen no reason why it shouldn't continue indefinitely.

It hadn't occurred to her that Aunt Muriel, too, would one day get fed up. It hadn't even occurred to her that by joining up with Clifford and the gang, she might not be pulling her weight, and keeping her end of the bargain which was to take advantage of the education offered, and fit herself for a good job like Aunt Muriel herself had done.

Now Sarah was having food for thought, and she felt rather mixed-up inside. The very young Sarah was protesting that Aunt Muriel couldn't do this to her, nor could Mr

Hilden. It wasn't fair just to be thrown out like that. But another, older Sarah was recognising that she deserved it, and there was a queer sort of excitement in life suddenly throwing one a completely new challenge. It might be a lot of fun standing on one's own feet, and not being beholden to Aunt Muriel any more.

Come to think of it, raced Sarah's thoughts, it had really been good of her aunt to do so much for her already. She had accepted it all as her due, yet now and again of late, she had felt vaguely uncomfortable, as though she ought to show gratitude, but didn't quite know how.

But if she stood on her own feet, there would be no need to feel like that. She'd be independent, and that would be a lot of fun. She'd get a salary, and be able to buy all sorts of exciting clothes and things. Not that her wardrobe was scanty ... far from it ... but Aunt Muriel had always supervised what she paid for, and considered a lot of new fashions to be made of absolute rubbish.

Sarah was unaware that her roving thoughts had caused her to stay silent for an unusually long time.

'Well?' Aunt Muriel was saying. 'How about it, Sarah? Are you willing to see Simon Demaine and have him decide whether or not you'll be suitable for this job? You'll still have to get it for yourself, you know. The Demaines aren't a charity organisation and won't be taking you on unless you're willing to work. Your stay won't be long if you don't suit them.'

'Of course I'll apply for it,' Sarah said, colour again in her cheeks, 'and I'll get it. I'm not a moron, Aunt Muriel.'

'I hope not, dear,' the older woman said mildly, then the soft expression was again in her eyes. 'Do your best, dear. I've every confidence that you'll do well and perhaps learn a great deal at Bonnygrass.'

'Is that the name of the place?'

'Yes. Bonnygrass House.'

'Oh, I like that!' Suddenly Sarah was smiling. 'I'd better look out my things, Aunt

Muriel, hadn't I?'

Muriel Duff nodded, biting her lip, then she forced back the small lump in her throat. She mustn't weaken now! Instead she reached into her desk drawer for her cheque book.

'Here's a cheque for you to cash,' she told Sarah, crisply. 'If there's anything you need, you must buy it, but I hope you'll add most of it to your savings, Sarah. It will be helpful if you have some money behind you in the bank.'

Sarah gasped at the amount, and looked at Aunt Muriel uncertainly. Then another look at the cheque loosened her tongue.

'Oh, Aunt Muriel, do you really want to give me all this? And I never say thank you, do I? I've t-taken it all for granted, haven't I? Yet I know you've been good to me. I... I'll pay it all back, I swear I will, after ... after I've earned a salary for a little while.'

Muriel Duff smiled through the sudden mist of tears.

'Don't be silly, child,' she said. 'Of course

24

I don't expect you to pay me back. I've been happy to do what I can for you. Nor...'

She stopped. She could hardly express disbelief that Sarah would be earning enough to have any left over for paying back! She would have to find that out for herself.

'On you go then, child,' she said, waving her hand. 'You've got a lot to do.'

For once in her life, Sarah took the initiative and leaned over the desk to give her aunt a hug and kiss, then she was gone, and Muriel Duff sat very still for a long time. Then she sighed and reached for her private notepaper and picked up her fountain pen.

'My dear Constance,' she began ... and the rest of the letter was private.

For Sarah, the journey to Kendal was not without interest. It was three years since she had paid a brief visit to the Lake District, and she had only the vaguest recollections of visiting Kendal to do some shopping.

Sarah had been born in Scarborough, and had lived there until her mother died, when she had gone to stay with Aunt Muriel in her spacious flat in Humberton. Sarah liked Humberton. She liked the hustle and bustle of the large city and had made quite a number of friends and had led a far from dull social life.

What would Kendal be like? she wondered. Would it be gay, too, and would there be lots of people calling on the Demaines? It was really rather exciting to make a new start, and to wonder about the future. That it no longer contained Clifford bothered her much less than she would have supposed.

But what if she didn't like the job? It was a long way to come back home to Humberton and Aunt Muriel ... who would probably be not at all pleased. It would be hard to admit failure in a short time. She must be prepared to stick it out for a month or two at least. Besides, it might really be a lot of fun...

Sarah's thoughts raced as she sat in the train and began to watch the changing landscape on the last lap of her journey. They were building a new motorway ... how nice! Maybe she could soon afford a car, if the job paid well, and it would be fun driving over to Humberton to see Aunt Muriel.

Sudden longing for her aunt bit into her heart and she had to control her tears with an effort. This was no way for a grown-up young woman to behave. What would Simon Demaine think of her if she appeared at the station streaming with tears?

It was a self-possessed young woman who stepped out of the train at Kendal and looked round for Simon Demaine. She had no idea what he looked like, and hadn't worried up until now about being able to find him. She scanned the people milling about her, young strong people in walking boots and anoraks, smart men and women of business, parents with their young children ... but no Simon.

Then she spun round as a hand was laid on her arm, and her heart pounded with excitement which turned to bewilderment. The man who approached her was a large, rather rough-looking young man with a cheerful red face and a soiled flat cap perched on his plentiful black hair.

'Miss Hudson?' he asked, and she nodded, then held out a timid hand which was shaken rather uncertainly.

'Mr ... Mr Demaine?' she asked tentatively.

'Mr Simon was busy, and I had to come into town with an order, miss,' the young man grinned. 'Thomas Roscoe, miss. I work in the nurseries ... Mr Simon's right-hand man, you might say.'

'Oh,' said Sarah, with some relief. Thomas Roscoe looked a cheerful, kindly young man, but he wasn't quite like the mental image she had formed of Simon.

'And Mrs Demaine?' she asked.

'Home at Bonnygrass, and she said she'd get your tea ready after your long journey. Is this all your luggage, miss? Best get home then 'fore they come looking for us. Train were late.'

Sarah followed Thomas out of the station to the car park, where he piled her luggage into a rather battered estate car, then helped her into the passenger seat.

'Home in a few minutes, miss,' he told her happily, and took off at a lick. The town was left behind in no time, and the car snaked down a rather narrow country road.

'I didn't know it … it was in the country,' said Sarah, looking round at green fields with hilly country beyond.

'Only the outskirts of Kendal,' said Thomas comfortably. 'Not real country like where I comes from. There you can tramp all day and not see a soul. Here the bus passes every quarter o' an hour, and folks is coming along to look at the gardens in their cars quite often. In high summer they fill up the roads goin' to the Lakes, most like.'

'I see,' said Sarah, and stopped talking abruptly as the estate car bumped into a narrow road through open gates, and up a short drive to Bonnygrass. A notice on the main road had pointed the way, and now Sarah looked eagerly at the lovely old house which was to be her new home, and the well laid out gardens to her left and beyond. A great deal of skill, planning and hard work had gone into making Bonnygrass very beautiful.

'It's ... lovely,' said Sarah softly, as she climbed out of the car.

'Sure is. Real nice,' agreed Thomas proudly. 'Me and Mr Simon, we done a fine job. The others, too, of course.'

'What others?'

'Oh, you'll meet them, miss, seein' as you'll be helping Mrs Demaine. She's a real nice lady is Mrs Demaine.'

But Sarah didn't answer, because the real nice lady was already coming out to welcome her with open arms.

'Sarah, my dear! It's years since I saw you, child. Why, you were only a little girl then, in long ringlet curls and a blue frock, I remember. It's strange to see you grown up.'

Sarah stared hard at the older woman. Somehow she had pictured someone tall and thin, rather like Aunt Muriel, but Constance Demaine was exactly the opposite, being short, rather plump, with fluffy grey curls and a round rosy face.

'How do you do?' Sarah said, holding out her hand, but Constance had decided to give her a bear-like hug. Sarah wasn't used to being hugged, but she decided she liked it, and hugged Mrs Demaine back.

'I'm glad you've come to help us,' Mrs Demaine was telling her as she led the way into the large old house. 'I couldn't get a girl at all, and how pleased I was when dear Muriel said you'd soon be looking for a position. I was relieved, my dear. I had Beattie for a while. She was a real treasure, but she got married, though who'd have thought it, goodness knows. She was a good girl, but very plain.'

For a moment she eyed Sarah doubtfully as she showed her up the stairs and into a pleasant bedroom.

'I hope you're strong enough for the job, dear. You aren't as tall as Muriel or Alice, are you? Your father was a big man, too…'

'You knew my father?' asked Sarah, her eyes suddenly alight with interest.

'Certainly I did. He was a fine young man and very talented. At least, he would have been if he'd lived. He was writing plays for television, you know.'

'I know.'

Sarah had been told this often by her mother, then by Muriel, and how he had been flying to New York because American television had become interested in his scripts, and how the plane had crashed.

'We'll talk about your father some time, if you wish,' said Constance, patting her shoulder. 'There's lots I can tell you about your parents when they were young. Now, dear, will you be comfortable in here? It's very quiet and you have a lovely view from this window. The bathroom is along at the end of the corridor, and if you hurry up, we can have tea as soon as you come downstairs. Tomorrow I'll take you all over the house and show you the layout. You'll need to know that. But you'd better have an early night tonight. Simon has gone to Lancaster, I'm afraid, and he's having dinner out, but he may be home before you go to bed. At any rate, you'll see him to-morrow.'

'Won't he have to approve of me … for the job, I mean?' asked Sarah.

'No, I don't think so,' Mrs Demaine told her cheerfully. 'He's leaving that to me. So long as we suit each other, Simon will be happy. Come down as soon as you're ready then.'

She ambled away, and Sarah closed her bedroom door thoughtfully. Simon, she decided, must be a real mamma's boy and no doubt let Mrs Demaine run his life for him.

Then she shrugged. Oh well, that probably didn't matter very much. She looked round the room, deciding that she liked it, and bounced up and down on the bed.

Mrs Demaine seemed harmless enough. No doubt it was going to be quite an easy, happy job for her. In fact, she could quite easily grow to love this place very much. It was really charming, and now that she could view the other side of the house, the lovely gardens and flowers were absolutely beautiful. Sarah loved flowers, and she decided she had fallen on her feet coming here.

Sarah wore a pretty black and white checked gingham dress with a wide scarlet belt when she came downstairs for tea, which proved to be a substantial meal, rather like the Scottish high tea.

'I thought this would be best,' Mrs Demaine explained, 'since there's only the two of us. I don't need to keep popping in and out of the kitchen.'

It was being served on a small table near the fire in the large spacious drawing room, which Sarah liked immediately, feeling at home among the bright chintz chair-covers, and admiring the lovely old furniture and thick Indian carpet.

'I like your drawing room,' she said shyly, to Mrs Demaine, and the older woman smiled with pleasure.

'Yes, it is rather nice, isn't it? Difficult to look after, but I hope you think it's well worth the trouble.'

'Oh, I do,' Sarah assured her earnestly, and her hostess nodded with satisfaction.

'Could you tell me about the gardens and the nurseries?' asked Sarah, as she helped herself to lovely fresh country butter.

'Well, of course, Bonnygrass used to be quite a large estate, but now we're down to about three acres, my dear. Simon decided he'd just have nurseries at first, then he thought a garden centre would be a good idea, so the grounds are laid out now like small individual gardens, so that people can come and choose which one would suit their home. You see?'

'That's a storming idea!' said Sarah, with enthusiasm, and Mrs Demaine blinked.

'Yes ... well, of course, Simon can design individual gardens, too. We're kept very busy now that winter is over, and there is a lot of work to be done ... office work as well as practical work in the gardens, and I expect to be very busy helping to show customers round and serve them in the shop. You understand? People also come to buy plants, shrubs and trees, and those are laid out in beds as well.'

Sarah nodded, and hoped she would be able to cope with all this office work. No doubt Simon would make allowances for her inexperience, she decided comfortably, and bit into a feather-light jam puff. Then she listened happily while Mrs Demaine went into a very detailed account of the nurseries.

'Are there many men working in the gardens?' she asked. 'I thought Thomas looked nice.'

'A very good worker, dear, though he's

usually out doing other people's gardens. There's also Jem Johnson, an elderly widower who lives in a cottage you can see from here, at the top of the hill. He's a bit morose, but very good with the flowers. You'll have to get to know Jem. And a young rascal called Bobby Mather who helps Thomas. Thomas says he's a good worker, if he keeps an eye on him, but if he sends him on an errand, then he doesn't come back for hours. He needs discipline, I think.'

Sarah was grinning. She guessed she knew Bobby's type very well, and had met one or two of them at College.

'Oh, and there's…'

The shrill ringing of the telephone bell cut off Mrs Demaine's speech, and she frowned as she went to answer it.

'Now, who can that be…?'

It was getting quite late. Sarah hadn't noticed the time slipping away, and now she felt very tired. She decided she would excuse herself and slip up to bed, and no doubt she would meet the rest of the staff tomorrow. They would be colleagues and she would want to get to know them all. She heard Mrs Demaine on the telephone.

'...very well, Ruth. Yes, I'll tell him when he comes in. That's right, dear ... see you tomorrow.'

She came back into the room, shaking her head slightly.

'Ruth Kirkham does take her job seriously, and I'm sure there is a meeting of some kind going at the Vicarage, too.'

'The Vicarage?'

'Yes, dear. I don't think I mentioned that Ruth is the Vicar's daughter. The Reverend John Kirkham, you know, but Mrs Kirkham is really very capable and helps to run the parish so that Ruth is not obliged to help too much and can follow her own affairs. You see, dear?'

Again Sarah nodded, and wondered if Ruth and Simon were special friends. She longed to know, but didn't feel bold enough to ask Mrs Demaine outright. After all, she hadn't even met Simon yet.

That was remedied fairly soon, because just as she said goodnight to Mrs Demaine, his key sounded in the lock and a moment later Simon walked in.

He was a very tall man, in his late twenties, with very dark hair and the rich dark complexion of the outdoor man. His eyes were almost black, and he bore no resemblance whatsoever to his small, plump mother, who was obviously very fond of him.

He wore a dark, well-cut suit, with sparkling white linen and a surprisingly gay tie, and Sarah felt her mouth go dry as he came forward to shake her hand, his stern face relaxing in a welcoming smile which made Sarah's heart turn over.

Clifford was forgotten. For her it seemed as though that moment had been carved out of time. Fervently she hoped that Simon was not engaged to Ruth Kirkham, or to anyone else, because she knew that no other man would ever hold her interest, or intrigue her, quite like this one.

'Sarah is just going to bed,' Mrs Demaine was saying. 'She's tired after her long journey and needs a rest. We're going to discuss her duties in the morning, aren't we, dear?'

Sarah nodded, feeling suddenly shy. She might have poor qualifications for being Simon's secretary, but she vowed in that moment that she would do her very best for him, and apply all her energies to learning the job.

'I ... I hope I'll be satisfactory,' she stammered shyly.

'I'm sure you will, dear,' Mrs Demaine told her happily. 'Simon will be as relieved as I am to have you here.'

'I certainly am ... er ... Sarah,' he told her, with a smile which sent Sarah upstairs on a cloud of air, her feet scarcely touching the carpet.

All of a sudden life had taken on a wonderful new meaning for her. She could see, now, that she had just been marking time at Art College and that everything was just beginning for her now.

Before going to sleep, she penned a glowing letter to Aunt Muriel, telling her how much she loved Bonnygrass already, and how nice Mrs Demaine and Simon were. She would leave it, stamped, on the hall table in the morning where Mrs Demaine had shown her.

Mrs Demaine had put a bottle in her bed, but had told her kindly that she would have to do it for herself after the first night.

Happily Sarah snuggled under the blankets, feeling drowsy and relaxed. It was quiet without the hum of traffic, and she listened to the night sounds of the countryside, an owl hooting, the faint sound of a train, one or two cars, and a rather unmelodious cat's concert, which she hoped would soon be over.

But minutes later she was sound asleep.

It was nine o'clock before Sarah got downstairs next morning. She had spent some time over her wardrobe, wondering what an efficient young secretary ought to wear these days, and finally deciding on a plain dark grey pinafore dress and a lovely buttercup yellow silk shirt, frilled at the neck and sleeves. She would have to be careful with the ink, decided Sarah, as she adjusted the frills over her wrists, and slipped her feet into dainty sandals. These she looked at doubtfully, wondering if she would be obliged to walk over the gardens, and if they had concrete paths or grass.

Then she shrugged. At least she would look nice when Simon first saw her again, she thought, brushing out her fluffy curls vigorously, and applying make-up and eyeliner.

This morning she found Mrs Demaine in the kitchen. This time she greeted Sarah rather more briskly than before.

'Oh, there you are, Sarah. I let you sleep late this morning, dear, since it's your first morning, but we keep early hours here and I shall want you down at seven-thirty for the first week, then seven after you've learned the routine and can take over from me. I've put an alarm clock in your room, so you can set it each night. Simon gets up at seven-thirty, you see, and starts at eight, and he likes a good breakfast.'

'Oh.' Sarah felt quite bewildered as she started to eat her cornflakes. 'Seven?' she repeated, not without dismay. 'That's awfully early for the office to open, isn't it?'

Mrs Demaine handed her a plate of bacon and eggs, then poured coffee for both of them.

'I'll just have a cup with you,' she decided, sitting down at the kitchen table opposite Sarah. 'Oh, the office isn't open till nine, dear,' she explained kindly. 'Ruth arrives about five to nine, and I think she deals with the post and that sort of thing first.'

'R ... Ruth?'

'I told you last night, Sarah, didn't I? Ruth Kirkham, the Vicar's daughter. She's Simon's secretary and generally keeps us all in order, though now that we're getting busy, I will have to help to receive people and show them round. That's why we needed you so badly, Sarah. I explained, didn't I, dear?'

Mrs Demaine drank her coffee, and Sarah began to have an odd sense of unreality.

'But... but what do I have to do?' she asked, half fearfully.

'Why, run the house, of course. Or help to run it would be more correct, because I'll still be supervising. We do have Mrs White twice a week for the heavy work, of course, but you'll find plenty to keep you busy. You'll need to cook breakfast for seven-thirty, then tidy up the house and keep the furniture well polished. I was so pleased you thought that worth while when you saw it last night, dear.'

Sarah's mouth hung open and she stared at Mrs Demaine as though mesmerised.

'The bedrooms need special care, too. Simon isn't very tidy, I'm afraid. Oh, and lunch is at one o'clock, and we all like a good meal, though not a very heavy one. Gardening can give one an appetite. Ruth goes home, and the men have an outhouse in which they eat their lunch. They like to bring their own lunch, you see, and they have facilities for making tea and warming up soup and pies, or whatever they've brought. At one time I tried to make a meal for them all, but it wasn't really successful. They're happier eating what they like and enjoying their own sort of conversation, you see, dear.'

'But...'

'That just makes the three of us ... you, Simon and myself, which will be easy for you. I shall keep an eye on ordering food and household requirements, of course, though you must write down anything which is getting low. We're hoping to offer light refreshments to customers in the summer time ... on little tables out in the gardens ... but that will be my job, not yours. Oh, and I shall take over in the house on Sundays, so you can have that day completely free.'

Sarah felt she was glad to hear it, though

utter disbelief had robbed her of speech. She couldn't be hearing right! She was supposed to be here to work with Simon, in the office, but Mrs Demaine obviously thought she'd come as ... as a domestic servant!

'There must be some mistake,' she said at length.

'No, Sarah. I shall certainly take over on Sundays. You are entitled to have Sunday to yourself, and a half-day, too, though we can decide which day would suit you later. And by the way, I rather think those pretty clothes won't be very suitable for housework. Perhaps you've got a light cotton dress which will wash easily? It's so easy to get stained in a kitchen when one is constantly being splashed with water, or hot fat from the cooker. I don't ask for cap and apron ... that would be *very* old-fashioned of me ... but I would like you to dress suitably, dear.'

Angry tears were rushing to Sarah's eyes.

'Mrs Demaine!' she cried. 'I tell you, there

46

must be some mistake. I... I understood I was to come here as ... as Simon's secretary!'

'Goodness!'

Sarah whirled round as the kitchen door opened, and a tall fair girl walked in closely followed by Simon. The girl had a neat head of honey-blonde hair, swathed into a roll at the back of her neck. She wore large horn-rimmed spectacles, which she now removed and dropped into a briefcase, showing a lovely, serene face with neat features and pale blue eyes. She looked very trim in a navy skirt and striped shirt blouse.

'Oh, hello, Ruth. This is Sarah Hudson, who's come to help me in the house,' began Mrs Demaine. 'Ruth Kirkham, Sarah dear.'

'How do you do?' said Sarah chokily, then turned to Mrs Demaine. 'I did *not* come to help you in the house!'

'Did I hear you say you'd come as Simon's secretary?' Ruth asked, her eyes gleaming with amusement. 'You didn't tell me I'd got the sack, Simon.'

Sarah looked at the tall dark man who stood looking down at her, his black eyes inscrutable. This morning he wore breeches and leggings, and a smart shirt, open at the neck, in a rich cinnamon colour which gave him a glowing appearance. Sarah swallowed and knew that her reaction to Simon last night had not been imagination. He was quite the most attractive man she had ever met, and she felt more bewildered than ever by the present situation.

She ... Sarah Hudson ... a domestic servant! Why, it was ludicrous. She was an artist ... a designer ... not even an office worker. She had never done domestic work in her life.

'What made you think you were my secretary?' Simon asked coldly, and Sarah swallowed.

'Aunt ... Aunt Muriel said that ... that...' She stopped.

'I thought I had explained to Muriel,' Mrs Demaine said in perplexity. 'I told her I couldn't get a girl here at all, and when she said you'd have to leave College without training … well, I thought that Alice's girl would know how to run a home. Alice and Muriel were well brought up girls, and knew how to do things properly. I assumed you'd be the same, Sarah.'

'Have you any training for office work?' Simon was asking quietly. 'Book-keeping? Typing? Shorthand?'

Sarah shook her head miserably, and lifted her chin as she again caught the gleam of laughter in Ruth Kirkham's eyes.

'I can answer the telephone,' she said evenly, and glared at Simon as he gave a hoot of laughter.

'You come here with no training,' he said, his eyes suddenly full of amusement, 'and expect to start in straight away as my … my secretary. This is a highly organised business, Miss Sarah Hudson, and I wouldn't let you near one of my rose bushes, even, without your knowing exactly what you're doing, much less my paper work or my telephone. Just what do you

49

think Bonnygrass is? Some sort of charity organisation, though I doubt you'd even be allowed to lay a finger on *that* without training!'

Sarah fell out of love with Simon immediately. In fact, she hated him, and only fierce pride kept her from dissolving completely into tears.

'I … I was misinformed,' she said stiffly, 'and … Aunt Muriel obviously didn't understand. I… I'll go and pack now.'

'And go where?' demanded Mrs Demaine.

'Look, Mother,' interrupted Simon quickly, 'I'll leave you to sort this out. Ruth and I must get through to the office. We've wasted far too much time already. Could we have some coffee, please, about eleven, when…' his eyes swept over Sarah's small stiff figure, and there was an unreadable gleam in them… 'When you've sorted out which one is going to make it.'

As the door shut behind them, Mrs Demaine turned again to Sarah.

'Do sit down, Sarah, and let's talk this over

sensibly. You need a job and we need help. Now tell me why we can't be of use to one another.'

'Not this job,' said Sarah, her lips stiff. 'I'm not a servant.'

'No one is these days,' interrupted Mrs Demaine firmly. 'The days for having a domestic servant, as you obviously mean it, have gone. Now we find someone of equal status to ourselves to give us help when we need it. That's how it's done these days, my dear. And you must know there's nothing lowly about running a home.'

'But ...' Sarah again forced back the tears. 'But I don't know anything about cooking! Nor about ... about polishing or cleaning, or anything.'

'You make your own bed, don't you?'

Sarah didn't know whether to nod or shake her head. In fact, Mrs Nesbit had always spoiled her shamefully and had kept her bedroom spotless. This morning, however, she had made her own bed, so she nodded reluctantly.

'Are you going to get married one day?' asked Mrs Demaine, going off at a tangent.

Sarah coloured furiously at the question, and thought again about Simon who had looked at her so superciliously when she had even been ready to fall in love with him.

'I doubt it,' she said coldly, and the older woman laughed.

'I doubt that reply,' she chuckled. 'You're very young yet, and very pretty. There are bound to be lots of young men after you, and what are you going to do when you have your own home? Leave your husband to do all the domestic chores as well as earning your daily bread?'

'I'm a designer, not a cook or bottle-washer,' said Sarah proudly. 'At least, I was going to be a designer...'

There was the pain of regret in her heart. What had happened to her? she wondered. Why was everything falling apart round her ears? Even Clifford, in jail for two weeks, seemed far away and unreal and she could only think of Aunt Muriel with fierce longing. She'd never really appreciated Aunt Muriel, thought Sarah miserably. Aunt Muriel had always looked after her and protected her, and they had loved each other even if they hadn't demonstrated that love. It had been deep down in her heart, and she was sure, in Aunt Muriel's, too.

But now she felt out in the cold, and rather frightened by all these twists and turns in her life.

'If you've got the brains to be a designer, you've got the brains to be a housekeeper,' said Mrs Demaine, standing up, 'and don't let anyone tell you differently ... it *does* take brains and initiative and ingenuity and a lot else besides to do this job properly, though I think it's a worthwhile job. Later I'll get Simon to show you round Bonnygrass, and I'm sure you'll feel proud to be part of it.'

Sarah said nothing, and Mrs Demaine gave her a sudden, unexpected hug.

'Come on, my love,' she said encouragingly, 'show us all what you're made of. We can work together for a week, and if an old woman like me can do it, so can a clever girl like you. You can't go running back to Muriel already, confessing failure. It wouldn't be fair to her, or to you. Don't make her any more disappointed in you. She's been good to you, hasn't she?'

'Very good,' said Sarah stiffly.

'Then pay her back a little. Make her proud to have helped rear a fine girl, and show us all that you've got the guts I think you have. Howard Hudson's daughter should have plenty of mettle.'

Howard Hudson's daughter watched the tips of her dainty sandals dancing jaggedly through a curtain of tears, but she bit her lip and blinked them away.

'All right,' she agreed, 'I... I'll give it a trial.'

'And we'll give you a trial, won't we?' Mrs Demaine said gently. 'Now off you go and find a simple dress. I'll wash up, but we must start to prepare lunch now. You can take coffee in to Simon and Ruth when you come back down.'

Sarah nodded and slowly climbed the stairs while the older woman watched her, a strange expression in her eyes. That night she, too, wrote a letter.

'My dear Muriel...'

CHAPTER TWO

The next week was the longest Sarah had ever known in her life. Her first impression of Bonnygrass had been that it was a charming, comfortable house, spacious yet easily manageable. But from that Tuesday morning, after she walked back downstairs clad in old jeans and a jersey with her oldest casual shoes, and joined Mrs Demaine in the kitchen, the house suddenly became as large and monstrous as a workhouse out of a novel by Dickens.

'You scrape those potatoes, dear, and prepare the cabbage while I beat up a meringue for the pudding. You'll need to know where everything is, but you can learn as we work together. I'll show you where all the cleaning materials are kept, too. Normally the bedrooms are done this morning, but since we're so late, it will have to be this afternoon.'

'All … all right,' agreed Sarah, rather shakily.

'I'll write out a work routine for you which will make things much easier so long as you stick to it,' went on Mrs Demaine. 'On Friday we go into Kendal for any special shopping, and the laundry calls on Monday morning. Mrs White comes on Mondays and Thursdays, and she keeps the windows clean and bright, and does the heavy scrubbing. After a little while you'll find it quite easy, dear. I did, and I'm a fat old woman three times your age!'

She laughed, and Sarah forgot her sulks to join in. Mrs Demaine was really very good-humoured, she thought, looking at the small plump woman whose white curls were a trifle disarrayed with exertion, which also brought a high rosy colour to her cheeks.

Lunch was a more talkative meal than Sarah would have supposed, though she felt rather hot and clumsy as she sat opposite

Simon. She knew he was a landscape architect and a lot of his work was done in the office, or out consulting his customers.

Sarah very much wanted to see round the gardens and greenhouses, but after the morning's humiliation she would rather have died than ask. Now that she had agreed to stay, Simon had accepted her casually, but remembered to thank her politely as she helped to serve the meal, her fingers all thumbs.

Mrs Demaine had left the coffee to her, and when she poured Simon's, he took a sip absently, then choked.

'My God, this is…' He stopped, seeing her scarlet face, and bit back what he was going to say.

'Sarah hasn't quite got used to everything yet,' Mrs Demaine excused her hurriedly. 'I've still got to show her how to use everything properly. I think she's made an excellent start, though, don't you?'

'Oh … er … of course,' Simon agreed, and the older woman smiled at her encouragingly. Almost against her will Sarah felt pleased, and smiled back rather timidly. She still had an unreal feeling about everything, as though it was all happening to someone else.

'I'll never settle down to this ... never!' she told herself, looking round the big kitchen which would soon be mainly her responsibility. Would she have to clean that electric stove? And wipe down the shelves? And the walls? Or would Mrs White do all that?

Before going back to the office after lunch, Ruth Kirkham called in, looking cool and well-groomed. She greeted Sarah pleasantly, almost making a point of being nice to her, and Sarah felt herself patronised.

In the afternoon Sarah and Mrs Demaine washed up together, then Sarah was shown over the whole house, this time viewing it all with new eyes. The lovely old furniture now took on the vast dimensions of miles of wood to polish. There was lots of parquet flooring with Oriental rugs and carpets, and even more delicate china ornaments, with enough brass and silver to keep her polishing for years.

Simon's bedroom was large and rather austere, with lots of books and a rather lovely small writing desk. It was all very neat, but only because Mrs Demaine kept it under control, or so she informed Sarah. Her own bedroom was rather pretty with a rose-coloured carpet and the palest of pink walls. There was a further three spare bedrooms, besides Sarah's.

'Don't you just put on dust covers?' she asked hopefully.

'Oh no, dear, not on this floor,' said Mrs Demaine, horrified. 'No, we do have visitors from time to time, and I like the bedrooms always to be available. One is inclined to neglect rooms which are just covered up. A quick clean once a week is all that's necessary, though. We've neglected things today, but they must have more attention next week.'

'Of course,' murmured Sarah.

There was only one bathroom, a vast affair with an old-fashioned bath, obviously made over from a bedroom. The lavatory was separate, but Sarah looked with dismay at the expanse of wall and floor, which she hadn't really noticed when she first made its acquaintance.

'There's also a cloakroom downstairs with a lavatory and washbasin,' Mrs Demaine explained.

'I've seen it,' Sarah assured her. 'Last night.'

'Ah yes. Now we'll go down and you can see the rooms we've missed.'

The first was Simon's study, which was again an expanse of polished wood to Sarah, with lots of books which no doubt gathered dust by the ton.

A small part of the house had been partitioned off to make a garden shop and office. It was here that Ruth worked as company secretary, and here that Mrs Demaine would now spend most of her time, serving customers and showing them round, or showing them where to go if they wished to browse by themselves.

Sarah had felt very resentful that she hadn't been thought competent enough to do that, but a few questions regarding her knowledge of gardens and flowers in general had soon shown her ignorance. Living in a flat had not helped to give her a built-in knowledge of the growing of flowers. She could recognise a rose when she saw one, but she couldn't distinguish between a hybrid tea and a floribunda. Nor could she describe what berberis would look like after it had flowered.

Sarah had been obliged to acknowledge that the job would suit Mrs Demaine much better than herself. But now she looked down the long broad corridors, and the rooms behind heavy oak doors, and wondered how long it would be before they grew slightly tatty-looking, the probable result of coming into her care.

'I won't let them,' she vowed with clenched hands. 'I won't let Simon, or Mrs

Demaine, or … or that Ruth have any cause to say one word!'

A strange fierce pride she hadn't known she possessed welled up inside her. She was as good, and perhaps a lot better, than any of them. She had just as many brains and intelligence, and if she really put her mind to it, she was sure she could be better than any of them.

It was that slow stirring of anger which drove her through the rest of the week, when many times she felt almost too tired to eat the meals she had helped to cook, or to admire the silver which she had polished. She had had no idea that housework could give one an almost permanent ache in the back, or use up one's last ounce of energy. Then, somehow, the week was up, and she was on her own.

For the first day or two, Sarah managed better than she had feared. Mrs Demaine had made it clear that she wouldn't be expected to do everything entirely on her own, and would have help as far as possible.

'But as we get busy, Sarah,' she explained, 'I shall have to leave the house to you because our customers are more important. You do see that, don't you, dear?'

Sarah nodded.

Mrs White had come on Monday morning, and had viewed Sarah with a motherly eye, but had accepted her without question. She had two daughters of her own, one with three small children and one with four, and as far as she was concerned, Sarah was getting off lightly with only this well-organised house to look after, and food to prepare for three people.

Mrs White changed the beds, and did the small laundry, then scrubbed out the bathroom and kitchen.

'I'd best do the curtains on Thursday, luv,' she suggested to Sarah, who looked blank, then agreed with her wholeheartedly. She dreaded being left with the curtains herself.

On Wednesday morning she received a letter from Aunt Muriel which should have cheered her up, but instead left her miserably depressed. She hadn't written since that first glowing letter which had been posted for her before she could retrieve it, and now Aunt Muriel was obviously relieved to hear that Sarah was so happy, and so enchanted with Bonnygrass.

'Oh, lor'!' thought Sarah mournfully, as she read it.

She had been up late that morning and had burned the toast and cooked fried eggs with brown frills round the edges. Simon had eaten his, but with evident lack of appetite and a rather glowering look in her direction. It seemed fantastic she had ever thought him attractive, and had even imagined she had fallen in love with him at first sight.

After breakfast the early morning haze had cleared like magic and the sun came up with a warmth unusual for early May. The day was beautiful with all the freshness of spring, giving Bonnygrass all the lovely bloom of youth.

Then the cars started to arrive.

In a secluded part of the gardens, Simon and Mrs. Demaine had organised about half a dozen small tables under gay umbrellas for serving light refreshments, and soon every table was full, and people were still coming.

'It's half-closing day for many towns, and some have the full day off,' explained Mrs Demaine to Sarah, as she boiled up coffee and made sandwiches. 'Could you help with this, dear?'

'But...'

Sarah had the lunch to cook, which was still a marathon task to her. Then, as Mrs Demaine hurriedly disappeared in the direction of the gardens, she shrugged and began to boil up more coffee and put buttered scones on a plate.

Then Ruth appeared.

'Where's Mrs Demaine?' she demanded. 'People are waiting.'

'She's in the gardens,' Sarah told her. 'We're coping as best we can, but all this is far too much.'

Ruth sighed deeply.

'Here, I'll do it,' she said, and took over. Somehow order was restored, the customers coped with efficiently, and Sarah found herself obeying all Ruth's instructions, and the morning righted itself.

'It's really just a matter of common sense, Sarah,' Ruth explained patiently. 'If you panic, things do get out of hand, but it can all be coped with quite easily if you think clearly, and get yourself organised.'

She smiled sweetly, and looked so cool and composed that Sarah felt the familiar lump rising in her throat. Her own appearance was frightful with fuzzy hair and a smut on her nose. She'd never learn, she thought mournfully, and decided she would give up now as she served up a hot casserole for lunch, followed by fruit salad and cream.

'Hm, this is good,' said Simon, and turned to smile at her.

'It's delicious, Sarah,' Mrs Demaine complimented her. 'I knew you were just the girl to help us, when you'd settled down and learned how to tackle the job. She's coping excellently, isn't she, Simon?'

'Of course she is.'

He was in an excellent mood, the morning having indicated that his garden centre was going to be an enormous success, and Sarah was quite surprised by the air of obvious relief he was showing, almost as though a burden was lifting.

She felt her heart doing strange things again, as his dark eyes smiled into hers, and her cheeks were warm as she poured a second cup of coffee, and offered the cheese and biscuits.

'Thank God for Ruth, though,' he said fervently, turning to his mother. 'If it weren't for her, I'd really have to think about more staff, and I honestly don't think we can run to more than casual help this year. We need all this business to cover everything.'

'She's wonderfully efficient,' agreed Mrs Demaine.

'Turn her hand to anything,' enthused Simon. 'We'll take on some students by another month when the universities and colleges break up for summer. They're always looking for jobs. Apart from that, I think we'll manage all right. Ah, here's Ruth now.'

The other girl sailed in, looking the very essence of spring in a crisp green and white suit, her hair gleaming like pale honey.

'Hello, everyone,' she beamed, including Sarah in her smile. 'Isn't it a marvellous day?'

Sarah nodded agreement, but she didn't feel at all marvellous. She was beginning to take an unreasonable dislike to Ruth Kirkham who had never done her any harm, and which, she was uncomfortably aware, was probably due to pure jealousy.

Sarah hadn't yet seen the gardens properly, having only paid short visits in the course of her duties. But Monday afternoon was rather quiet, and after the usual busy morning in the house, Sarah had an hour or two to herself while Mrs White got on with her cleaning jobs.

'I'll show you round, Sarah,' Mrs Demaine decided. 'Put on a cardigan, dear. There's a colder wind blowing today, and you mustn't catch cold.'

Sarah nodded, and rushed upstairs two at a time. She had been looking forward to seeing round the garden centre.

Out in the grounds it was, indeed, rather chilly, but Sarah was too interested to notice. The gardens were laid out neatly behind the house, and showed a variety of delightful ideas, showing how flowers could be planted to the greatest advantage. There were rose bushes everywhere, though some of them not yet in bloom. At the moment it was the lovely azaleas, camellias and laburnum trees like droplets of sunshine which gave colour and perfume to the gardens.

'Let's go through the greenhouses first, Sarah,' Mrs Demaine suggested. 'It's so nice to be in out of the cold, if you know what I mean.'

In fact, it was rather suffocatingly warm to Sarah, as she watched Mrs Demaine carefully closing the door.

'We mustn't leave it open, dear,' she warned. 'That's the first rule you must learn about Bonnygrass.'

Sarah forgot the heat as she turned to see Thomas Roscoe walking towards her, a grin on his cheerful face. She had seen little of Thomas since he drove her out to Bonnygrass as he worked away a great deal, but now he greeted her with a beaming smile.

'Hello, Miss Hudson. Want to see round?'

'Yes, please. Oh....!'

As she stared along the greenhouses at the variety of coloured blooms, the exclamation came involuntarily from her lips. She had always loved flowers, but had never before seen them growing in such profusion. Thomas reeled off long-sounding Latin names, with more common names thrown in.

'Isn't that a vine?' she asked, when they

reached the other end of the greenhouse.

'That's mainly for our own use, dear,' Mrs Demaine explained, 'though we hope to sell some of the grapes with the refreshments this year. But you'll be able to have plenty of good black grapes later in the year, and Thomas here enjoys making his own wine, don't you, Thomas?'

'Sure do,' he agreed. 'Miss Hudson can have some of it if it won't knock her flat on her back.'

Sarah grinned and assured Thomas that it wouldn't.

'You haven't tasted it yet, dear,' put in Mrs Demaine, her eyes twinkling.

Sarah spoke to several workers, each busy with a particular job. Young Bobby Mather grinned at her cheekily as he potted up some plants, while Jem Johnson straightened up from a bed of young rose bushes to smile at her with dignity and reserve. Sarah liked and admired Jem, and hoped to visit him one day in his cottage. He had diffidently given her the invitation when she talked to him one day in the kitchen after he had brought round the vegetables.

'It looks a lovely little house,' she told him, peering out of the kitchen window. 'Like something out of a fairy tale. Do you live there all by yourself, Mr Johnson?'

'Aye,' he replied, rather heavily. 'Since my wife died. It were a bonny place then, though I tries to keep it nice for her sake, like. Er … if you want to see it close to, miss, come walking over one Sunday and we can drink a cup o' tea together. You goes up that road, see, and take the path first to your left.'

'I'd like that, Mr Johnson,' Sarah said shyly.

Now she resolved she would make the journey very soon as Jem straightened to smile at her. She felt that he was a good man who could be a friend. Bobby Mather made her laugh, too, with his impudent wink, though she would have to keep an eye on young Bobby, she decided, as she and Mrs Demaine walked slowly round the gardens.

'It's all so beautiful,' she said, looking at the back of the house, and the patio to the left, in front of which the gay tables had been set out in a secluded part of the gardens. 'You and Simon must be very proud to own such a lovely place.'

'Yes,' agreed Mrs Demaine, though there was an odd note in her voice, and Sarah looked at her closely, seeing a shadow on her face.

'It's a wonderful project,' went on Sarah, 'and you must be happy seeing it such a success.'

Again Mrs Demaine nodded, then sighed deeply.

'I ... I suppose I ought to tell you, Sarah, though there's no reason why I should, other than that you're Alice's girl and Muriel's niece. Bonnygrass...' She stopped for a moment to get her breath. 'Bonnygrass is carrying a mortgage at the moment. Simon ... Simon and I have been rather worried over it.'

Sarah was astonished.

'A mortgage!' she echoed. 'But … but I thought it had been in the family for years and years.'

'It has,' Mrs Demaine assured her, 'but when Simon's father died, I'm afraid he left rather a large amount of debts. Oh, it wasn't his fault, poor darling. He just wasn't used to looking after money, and wouldn't let me take over. He was old-fashioned about women and thought we oughtn't to have a brain in our heads apart from managing the housekeeping. I used to worry a little, as there were small signs that he wasn't managing as well as he might, but I didn't realise the real position till he died.

'Luckily Simon was almost trained, and we had an awfully good friend in Colonel Vause who lived in that big house you can see in the distance there, through the trees. It's a maternity home now, converted just recently. Anyway, the Colonel seemed well and strong then, and he gave Simon a private mortgage on the house to start him off on the garden centre. He and John had always been such good friends, and the Colonel was most insistent that Simon should accept, and not just let Bonnygrass go.

'But the Colonel died last year, and some sort of cousin has inherited and has been selling up the estate. He's taken over Simon's mortgage, too, and it would suit him very well to have us out and this ground sold to the property developers.

'So you see, dear, that it's an anxious time for Simon and me, as we must make a success of the business or lose our home. I … I think that would be very hard. We … I wrote to Muriel as she's an excellent solicitor and just put the facts to her so that she could explain to me clearly how we stand. I can grasp things very well if they're put simply, but I find the law very confusing at times.'

Sarah nodded.

'That's how Muriel told me… I mean, that's how she knew I needed someone like you, dear. You see?'

'I see,' nodded Sarah again.

'And I hope you'll respect my confidence, Sarah. Simon wouldn't want me to burden you, a young girl, with our troubles, but I feel you'd understand everything better if you knew all the facts. We're rather understaffed, my dear, and that's why I like to do my bit, and why we expect rather more from you, perhaps, than we ought. But I knew I could depend on Alice's girl and Muriel's niece.'

Sarah didn't know what to say. She wished she could give Mrs Demaine a big hug and tell her not to worry about a thing, and she'd run the house on oiled wheels and allow the older woman to help out with the business. Only she knew that she still had the job very much on top of her, and it could very easily be too much for her.

Yet she had grown fond of Simon's mother and hated to see her worried. Now she must strive harder than ever to make a success of her job … and how awful she would feel if it did turn to chaos!

As they walked past the rest of the gardens towards the house, Sarah paused for a last look.

'Simon must surely sell lots of gardens,' she said reflectively. 'They are really gorgeous, aren't they? Did he design all of them?'

Mrs Demaine nodded.

'He's having lots of orders for individual designs, too ... people who feel they'd like something to fit in with their own property.'

'I see,' said Sarah. 'Oh, look, what's that?'

As they neared the house she pointed to a peculiar-looking tree with furry twisted branches which amused her at first glance.

'That's a monkey puzzle,' Mrs Demaine explained. 'Do you like it?'

'It's funny,' giggled Sarah, then stared at it again, doubtfully. The long twisted furry branches reminded her of large furry spiders and she shivered a little.

'I don't know if I like it,' she said honestly, 'but I can imagine some people would find it sort of ... different.'

Inside the house they found Ruth efficiently setting out a tray for herself and Simon.

'Oh, Ruth dear,' said Mrs Demaine guiltily, 'I'm sorry. We forgot the time, Sarah and I. I was just showing her round all the gardens.'

'That's all right,' said Ruth, with a quick, very bright smile. 'Sarah must see the gardens by all means. It was no trouble for me to get the coffee.'

As she sailed out with the tray, Sarah wished Ruth didn't make her feel so inadequate. She looked apologetically at Mrs Demaine, whose eyes suddenly twinkled as they met hers.

'We've been backsliding, Sarah,' she said wryly. 'We'd best get back to work.'

On Friday Sarah had a list of new provisions requiring to be ordered. 'Who does the small shopping in Kendal?' she asked carefully, and Mrs Demaine was about to reply and then paused.

'Would you like to go,' she asked, 'if I tell you which shops?'

'Oh, I'd love to,' said Sarah. 'How do I go there?'

'Thomas will take you in the estate car. He goes into Kendal every Friday just shortly after lunch and you can arrange to meet him somewhere so that he can bring you home. It is only odds and ends, dear, and I will order all the rest by telephone and have it delivered.'

Sarah sang that morning as she polished the old furniture in the sitting room, though she looked at it all rather doubtfully when she had finished. It should have shone beautifully as the patina was wonderful and came up beautifully when she worked at it with Mrs Demaine, but now it looked a trifle smeary, and she gave it all another rub which didn't seem to do much good at all. It smelled nice – the polish having a lavender perfume. She turned to pick up her duster as Ruth poked her head round the door.

'Have you seen Mrs Demaine, Sarah?' she asked.

'She went out just a short time ago,' Sarah told her, and again tried to rub up the front of the sideboard.

'Heavens!' said Ruth, coming further into the room. 'What have you done with that?'

'Polished it,' said Sarah briefly. 'It's on my routine list for this morning, and shopping for this afternoon.'

'Let me see,' Ruth commanded her. 'You've sprayed on too much polish and let it dry, you ninny! Honestly, Sarah, you are an idiot. Didn't you read the instructions? Spray on just a little, use clean dusters and rub. These ones are for the floor, by the way.'

'Oh, 'eck,' said Sarah, with dismay. 'Whatever will I do?'

'We'd better do something,' said Ruth, with decision. 'This is all good antique furniture. I think Mrs Demaine must be off her head letting you near it, Sarah.'

'Near what?' asked Simon as he came in

the door. 'Did you find Mother, Ruth?'

'No, I found Sarah spraying polish all over the furniture and letting it dry on. It's going to need some rubbing off.'

Simon's eyes glittered.

'Well, let her get on with it, Ruth,' he said with annoyance. 'We haven't time to bother with the furniture.'

'We must,' said Ruth firmly. 'It's too good to spoil, but leave it to me, Simon. I'll see to it.'

Simon looked daggers at Sarah.

'You go back to the kitchen, Sarah,' Ruth told her crisply. 'I can handle this by myself, and I'll come back early from lunch, Simon, and get that estimate finished in time. Don't worry … it'll be ready.'

Sarah's cheeks were crimson as she turned to march off to the kitchen. She felt so humiliated she was ready to cry, but now that she looked at the tin, she saw that it warned her not to use too much polish, and polish off immediately.

Lunch was a silent meal. Even Mrs

Demaine was reproachful as she was proud of her lovely old furniture, then she sighed deeply.

'I suppose it was my fault,' she confessed. 'I should have shown you several times, Sarah. It didn't occur to me you'd become confused. I ... I thought Muriel's furniture was also well cared for.'

'Mrs Nesbit looks after it,' Sarah told her miserably.

'But didn't you ever help?'

Sarah bit her lip. She had done nothing in the flat. It was only now she was realising there must have been quite a lot of work in looking after the place, which she had just taken for granted.

'It's no use, is it?' she asked miserably, as she sat over her coffee. 'I'm no good as a housekeeper at all. I... I'd better leave.'

Her voice wobbled, because suddenly she didn't want to. Suddenly she wanted a share in helping to make Bonnygrass a success.

Simon was glowering at her, and she looked straight back at him. She didn't know how she felt about him, feeling furious with him sometimes because he had the ability to humiliate her, and at others feeling an odd sweetness catching at her heart when he smiled at her, and gave her a word of praise.

Besides, there was Mrs Demaine. It seemed a long time since Sarah knew a mother's love. She and Aunt Muriel loved each other, but it was a love which was well under the surface. Now she was beginning to love this older woman, feeling warmed by her comfortable and understanding ways. And even Bonnygrass, with the lovely gardens and spacious old house, was taking hold of her heart.

'Do you want to run away?' Simon was asking, rather roughly. 'You've only been here a week or two and we realise you're just learning, though for heaven's sake, ask when you don't know. And don't go thinking you do know, when you don't. Do you really want to throw in the sponge?'

Sarah shook her head. 'Not ... not yet,' she confessed.

'Then get ready for town,' Simon advised her crisply. 'You can come with me this afternoon. Thomas is having to take the larger van to Penrith. Only do get cleaned up, young woman. Your hair is like a floor-mop.'

Sarah's tears turned to anger. Simon would be a mess, too, if he'd had the same sort of morning she'd had! It was all very well for Ruth, sitting in the office all day and talking so crisply and efficiently to people on the telephone, but it was a different matter having to cook and clean and polish, especially when she made a mess of it.

'I'm sure Sarah will look very nice,' said Mrs Demaine to Simon. 'We'll have salad for tea, dear, then you can feel free this afternoon and not hurry back. I shall have to arrange for you to have more time off.'

'Be ready at two-thirty sharp,' Simon told her as he walked out. 'I don't wait for you if you aren't.'

'All right,' agreed Sarah meekly.

'Will your shopping take long in Kendal?' asked Simon, as he edged the estate car down the drive and into the main road.

'No, I don't think so.' Sarah eyed the list, and the careful instructions as to how to make her purchases. Mrs Demaine had explained that this was because she didn't yet know the shops, but Sarah felt, uncomfortably, that it was probably because Mrs Demaine was taking no chances, and thought her liable to make a mess of it otherwise.

'Read it out,' commanded Simon, and she did so. 'Right,' he said. 'I'll help you, then you can sit in with me while I run over to Grange on business.'

'Grange? Do you mean Grange-over-Sands? But I'll be expected back...'

'Don't be silly,' Simon said, rather roughly, then his tone was suddenly gentle. 'Have we been too hard on you, Sarah, and made you feel like a kitchenmaid in Victorian times? We forget, you see, that you're not one of the family, and that you ought to be quite happy to work for Bonnygrass all day and every day.'

'Oh, but I do want to work for Bonnygrass,' Sarah assured him, 'if it will help to keep that nephew or cousin of Colonel Vause off your back.'

'What do you know about that?' asked Simon in a cold, rather angry voice, and Sarah realised she'd put her foot in it.

'N ... nothing really,' she stammered.

'Mother had no right to pass our worries on to you, so forget it, will you?'

'Oh, don't be angry with her.' Sarah was rather distressed. 'She's ... well, she didn't mean to tell me, and I don't want you being rotten to her because she let it out.'

'Rotten to her?' echoed Simon. 'Am I rotten to people, Sarah?'

'I don't suppose you can help it,' she told him kindly. 'Having things on your mind, I mean. But I like your mother ... in fact, I love her, really, and I don't want her upset.'

'No, I see,' said Simon, a rather odd note in his voice. 'Well, let's park the car and get that shopping done.'

As he helped Sarah from the car, he noticed that she certainly hadn't neglected her appearance. She was wearing her lovely soft white wool suit, and her dark curls had been brushed neatly, close to her head. Simon felt vaguely irritated and out of sorts with himself as he marched Sarah firmly towards the shops. He had never been anything else but considerate towards the girl, yet here she was accusing him of being rotten ... rotten! to her, and his mother!

The shopping was done in no time, and piled into the back of the car, and Simon took the A6 towards the turn-off for Barrow, a silent Sarah sitting demurely beside him.

'Do we go through the Lake District?' she asked.

'Only the southern tip,' he told her. 'Why? You've been to the Lake District, haven't you?'

She shook her head. 'Only a brief visit, and I didn't see very much of it, so I don't really know it.'

'Not know the Lake District!' cried Simon. 'We'll have to put that right. I thought you'd have known it well.'

'I presume you know the east coast well?' asked Sarah rather tartly. 'Scarborough ... Hull...?'

'Well ... no ... touché,' murmured Simon. 'It's just that...'

'I know,' nodded Sarah, and again Simon felt discomfited.

'Would you like to come with me to see some of the Lakes on Sunday?' he asked carefully. 'We could go to Lake Windermere first, then on up to Ulverston.'

'I'm going to visit Jem Johnson in his cottage on Sunday, for tea,' Sarah told him flatly. 'His wife was clever with her hands, and did lots of embroidery, and Jem wants to show it to me. It's very nice of you to ask me, but I shan't be able to come with you.'

'Oh,' Simon said.

He felt unusually disappointed, and a trifle surprised. Jem tended to keep himself to himself since Janet Johnson died. He must have taken to Sarah to invite her to visit him so soon.

He glanced at her profile, seeing the neat little nose, the firmly pointed chin, and the curls clustering about her small ears. Probably she was just the kind of daughter Jem would have wanted, but never had.

Illogically, however, he felt irritated again that she hadn't leapt at his offer of a date, and in fact, already had one.

'Sunday week, then,' he suggested. 'Oh, lord, no! I'm going out with Ruth that day. It will have to be the second Sunday in June. Will that do?'

'If I'm still here,' said Sarah, 'I'll be glad to come with you.'

'If you're still here,' he repeated grimly.

'Oh, look!' she said. 'Isn't it pretty?' They had passed through a lovely village which caught at Sarah's heart, and she enjoyed the scenery till they reached Grange.

'He's a spare key,' said Simon. 'You can wander about while I see the owner of a flower shop, but be back in half an hour.

We'll have tea here before we go home.'

'All right, Simon,' said Sarah, smiling with genuine pleasure.

She loved Grange, and spent some time looking in shop windows, then looking out to sea, which she often missed quite a lot. In an odd sort of way it reminded her of Scarborough, perhaps because she was now looking down on the calm blue of the sea from a high vantage point, and there was a place in Scarborough where she could do just the same.

Sarah breathed deeply of the tangy air, and felt strangely full of well-being. Her body was getting used to the physical effort involved in running a home, and the exercise was probably doing her good, she admitted honestly.

And it was nice to be having tea with Simon, she decided, as they sat in an attractive tea-room while he ordered tea, sandwiches and cakes.

'I love it here,' Sarah said simply.

'I'm glad.'

Simon's black eyes suddenly smiled into hers. It had been a profitable journey from his point of view, and he had made some excellent business arrangements. He looked lots younger when he wasn't scowling and worried, thought Sarah ... much more like her first impression of him when she had been prepared to fall madly in love with him. She blushed, now, when she thought of her first sight of him.

'Penny for them, Sarah,' laughed Simon, and she blushed even more.

'Not worth it.'

'Oh, come now.'

'I was thinking you look more like you did when I first saw you,' she said honestly. 'I thought how handsome you were, and how I could easily fall in love with you. Though, of course, that didn't last long.'

Simon felt devastated by her clear-eyed honesty, but had to admit he had asked for it. It was his turn to colour furiously.

'What a funny child you are,' he told her lamely.

'I suppose so,' agreed Sarah pensively, 'though I'm not really such a child. I'm nineteen, only ten years younger than you.'

'It seems a lifetime,' said Simon dryly. 'Do you want yet another cake before we go or have you had enough?'

She eyed a delectable cream puff.

'Just one more,' she decided. 'How about you, Simon?'

'No, thanks. I've had quite enough for one day.'

They drove home in silence.

CHAPTER THREE

On Sunday afternoon Sarah walked up the hill to the little cottage which belonged to Jem Johnson. She wore her cinnamon-coloured suit with matching shoes and handbag in honour of the occasion, feeling that Jem would appreciate that she had dressed up.

It was a lovely little house. Though the rooms were small, they were bright and cosy, with comfortable chairs and good carpets. It was surprisingly neat and tidy.

'Oh, you *do* keep it nice, Jem,' Sarah told him, when he showed her over the cottage. 'You'd be a much better housekeeper at Bonnygrass than I am.'

'We all have to learn, Miss Sarah,' Jem told her smiling, 'though from what I see, you aren't making such a poor job now.'

'I am learning,' admitted Sarah. 'I've even written to my aunt to tell her what I'm doing. She thought I was going to be a secretary!'

'Best off leaving that to Miss Kirkham,' Jem advised. 'She's a great organiser, that one. She runs the Youth Club, too, Miss Sarah, and it's a wonder she hasn't roasted you into joining up with her. She's a rare one for roping folks in to help out with the good works.'

'I don't think I want to join just yet, Jem,' Sarah said slowly.

The Youth Club made her think of Clifford and all her other young friends at Art College, and she often felt uncomfortable, remembering. She must have been an awful fool, she decided, throwing away her chances as she had done. No wonder Aunt Muriel had been fed up.

Jem allowed her to help set the table for tea, and she admired the lovely embroidered cloth.

'One o' my wife's,' he told her proudly.

'After tea I'll show you what else she sewed.'

It was a delightful farmhouse tea with scones, fresh butter and honey, and slabs of cheese on fresh crusty bread.

'Eat up, Miss Sarah,' Jem advised her, cutting a large slice of rich fruit cake. 'You're too thin. I thought so when I first saw you that there's a young lady that's far too thin for her own good. My wife was a well-built woman ... a fine, bonny woman.'

His voice was sad, and Sarah looked at him sympathetically.

'You'd no children, Jem?'

'Only one lad, but he died when he were a bairn.'

After tea Sarah admired the beautiful embroidery which Jem had folded away in a well-lined drawer scented with lavender.

'Her heart were bad,' Jem explained, 'so she had to spend long hours sitting, and that's how I got good at running the house and cleaning it up, though I've a good neighbour helps me at times. Janet told me what to do, and saw I did it all proper like.

And I bought her things to sew and nice pleasant gentle books to read ... no kitchen sink stuff for Janet ... and she were content.'

'Oh, look at that picture!' cried Sarah, going up to view a lovely embroidered picture on the wall. It showed a graceful fawn, its neck beautifully curved, reaching up to eat leaves from an overhanging tree. Janet Johnson had captured all the charm of an idyllic scene.

'She's sewed it exquisitely,' Sarah said, looking closely at the tiny, neat stitches.

'Aye, she reckoned that were a nice picture,' said Jem, delighted at her appreciation, 'and I reckon my Janet would have liked you to have that, Miss Sarah.'

'Oh, Jem!' Sarah turned swiftly and shook her head in dismay. 'You mustn't give it away, or let it go out of the house,' she protested. 'Why, it's one of your treasures.'

'You don't think I'd offer you rubbish, do you?' Jem asked, a trifle dryly, and Sarah was afraid she had offended him.

'I would treasure it always,' she told him softly.

'Then it's yours, Miss Sarah,' he said, and lifted down the picture, going into the kitchen for a duster to polish it up. 'I framed it myself.'

'It's ... beautiful, Jem,' said Sarah sincerely.

Before she left, Jem suddenly turned the subject towards Bonnygrass.

'It's getting to be a fine place,' he told her. 'Mr Simon's worked hard on it. It's better now than it were in his father's day, though I often thought he could have profited by it instead of just living in it. It ... it would be a pity if anything happened to it now.'

'Happen? Oh, you mean...?'

Sarah bit her lip. She had no idea if Jem and the others knew about the mortgage on the estate, and her thoughtless tongue had already given her away to Simon. Jem was a loyal worker, she was sure, but it wasn't up to her to gossip.

Jem, however, was looking slightly anxious.

'That Raymond Vause is very free with his money,' he told her, in an off-hand sort of voice.

'Free with his money? Raymond…? You mean the man who inherited the Vause estate?'

'Aye, the young rascal who's converting the lot into money. That's all he cares about … getting the money for it. He's living in one of them luxury flats at Bowness and has some sort of commercial scheme to attract the trippers, from what I hear. That's where the money's going to go.'

'Oh,' said Sarah.

'He's too free with it at times, Miss Sarah,' Jem said again, and she looked at him, puzzled.

'Is he?' she asked. 'What's that got to do with Bonnygrass, Jem?'

'Happen nothing, happen plenty,' he told her helpfully. 'You're a friend o' the Demaines, aren't you, Miss Sarah? A young relative, Mrs White thought.'

'Oh no, not really,' she corrected. 'My

parents and Aunt Muriel were friends of Mrs Demaine's.'

'That's good enough. You'll be like one o' their own folks, I dare say, when they brought you here to stay with them. You just watch out for young Vause, then. He's a rascal, Miss Sarah. He'd do Mr Simon a nasty trick, quick as look at him, though I'll be doing me best to watch out for him, that I will.'

Sarah wanted to ask what she could do about it, but decided just to accept all that Jem had told her. She began to wonder if her invitation to tea had all been for some mysterious purpose which was going on in Jem's head. She could make little of the hints he was giving her, and obviously he didn't want to be drawn. Was that why he hadn't gone to Simon or Mrs Demaine? They would have demanded to know more, yet perhaps Jem was the type to keep his own counsel, but had felt they ought to be put on their guard, so he was doing it through her.

For a moment she felt disappointed that her visit to Jem's cottage might have been prompted by an ulterior motive, then she looked down at the lovely picture, and knew that Jem liked her for her own sake.

'I'll remember what you've told me, Jem,' she said softly, and he beamed with relief.

'I knew you'd a head on your shoulders, Miss Sarah,' he told her. 'Just remember ... that one is free with his money.'

But what did Raymond Vause do with his money when he was 'free with it'? wondered Sarah as she walked home. Ought she to tell Simon, or Mrs Demaine? They would get it out of her where she had heard the remark, then Simon would put Jem on the carpet.

Sarah visualised Jem's reproachful eyes on her, and decided to say nothing at all. She knew nothing about anything at the moment, only that Simon was working hard to keep the mortgage paid, and they were all willing to work hard and help him.

She took the back way into the house, through a small wicket gate and walked down through the gardens. As she passed the monkey puzzle, its twisted arms seemed to reach out to her, and Sarah almost backed away. It was stupid to be put off by a small tree, she told herself angrily. Really, it was quite a nice little tree, and very unusual. She would have to take a proper view of it, and of everything else.

Slowly Sarah made her way indoors, then went straight up to her room. The picture frame also had a leg on it, and she was able to place it on a chest of drawers. It would always remind her of a woman who had got the most out of life, in spite of chronic ill-health, she thought. It would be a real inspiration to her.

But that night she began to wonder about Raymond Vause, who was far too free with his money.

The days began to roll past, and suddenly it was June and the scent of roses was everywhere, while the gardens took a new dimension, glorious in their beauty.

'They're absolutely wonderful,' said Sarah to Mrs Demaine, as she looked at all the different varieties. 'I've always loved roses. I often think I have a favourite, then I see another and another, so I know I just love all of them.'

Mrs Demaine smiled at her enthusiasm.

'Yes, they are lovely, aren't they? I suppose I've looked on them too much as goods in our shop window to love them for their own sakes. We're going to need all we can grow this year. Many people are coming out to the garden centre just for the sake of buying flowers now.'

'I know,' agreed Sarah, rather ruefully.

Of late she had been left with the house very much on her own hands, but luckily she was beginning to take it in her stride. Even Ruth, poking around to check up on her, hadn't been able to find fault too much, and Simon had eaten the meals she served up with enjoyment and a quick word of thanks. He was looking rather tired, but it was physical fatigue, rather than mental, and the small lines of worry etched on his brows were smoothing a little. It seemed to Sarah that he might be gradually winning his battle, and she felt proud to be helping in her own way.

'We're taking on one or two students now,' he informed his mother over lunch. 'We've advertised in the *Gazette,* so no doubt they'll be rolling up in a day or two. I was wondering if those attic bedrooms would do for them, if they can't travel easily.'

The old house had a third floor which wasn't in use at the moment, though the rooms could be made ready whenever they were required.

'Well...' Mrs Demaine looked dubious, glancing unhappily at Sarah. 'They *could* be used, I suppose,' she said slowly, 'but it might mean extra work for Sarah who has quite enough already.'

'Oh, we'd have to get someone to help her,' Simon assured them. 'I wouldn't expect you to run after three or four young students, Sarah.'

'Thank you,' she told him dryly.

'We' could go and look at them, Sarah dear, and see what you think. You'll know better than I whether students would be comfortable there.'

Sarah remembered some of the accommodation which had housed Clifford and other members of their gang.

'I don't need to look,' she told them. 'They'll be comfortable.'

Later, however, she and Mrs Demaine climbed the second flight of stairs which opened out into a lovely long low room with two small dormer windows. Some old chairs and other pieces of furniture had been covered in dust-sheets, and these were soon removed.

'This could be a sitting room for them,' suggested Mrs Demaine. 'There are three more bedrooms. It used to be the servants' quarters in the days when we had servants.'

'I thought you'd still got one,' said Sarah, smiling a little.

'Not you, dear,' the older woman hastened

to assure her. 'You're like one of the family.'

Oddly enough she felt like one of the family. She had never felt so much at home with anyone as she felt with Simon's mother.

It was fun, even, going through the bedrooms and checking on how much required to be done to make them habitable. They were a trifle bare, but they had good lino on the floor, with one or two good but faded rugs, and the walls were surprisingly clean.

'They were done up five years ago,' Mrs Demaine explained, 'but rooms do keep clean out at Bonnygrass. The air is very pure, you know, dear.'

'I know,' agreed Sarah.

She had been thankful for that. Bonnygrass would have been impossible for her in a smoky atmosphere.

'Well, what do you think?' asked Mrs Demaine.

'I think Simon ought to pick his students carefully,' warned Sarah as they walked back downstairs. 'Most are good and hard-working, though there are the few who don't appreciate when they're well off. I know. I was one of them.'

'Do you regret not taking up an artistic career?' asked Mrs Demaine. 'Now you're looking at it all in retrospect? Maybe it's not too late, you know, Sarah. Maybe you could pick up the threads again when you feel ready to do so.'

Sarah shook her head.

'Well, I'm not ready yet, and I doubt very much if I could go back to train again. Anyway, I've got a job now, haven't I?'

'You certainly have. Simon and I are very glad to have you. But if we're going to have these young people around, we'll need to organise some help. I wonder if Mrs White would have more time on her hands now.'

Sarah was quite happy with that arrangement. Mrs White decided she could come daily during the summer months, and together she and Sarah tidied up the attic bedrooms.

'It won't matter if they are bare, luv,' Mrs

White remarked, as they surveyed their handiwork. 'Them young limbs will have the rooms knee-deep in rubbish in no time. I know. I reared a couple myself. Don't worry, though, luv, I'll see to them and keep them in order. They won't take no liberties wi' me.'

'Oh, that would be fine, Mrs White,' said Sarah gratefully.

It was only two days later when the first student turned up, knocking lightly on the office door, and walking straight in, much to Ruth's annoyance.

'You should wait till you're invited in,' she said severely, looking rather haughtily at the young man whose long hair merged with a beard and thin drooping moustache. He wore blue jeans, a tartan anorak and rather scruffy-looking brown boots, but he was clean, decided Ruth, her eyes sweeping over him.

'Oh ... I thought it was a garden centre and shop.'

'This is the private office. The shop is through that door.'

'Never noticed. I was looking for Miss…'

'Kirkham,' broke in Ruth. 'I take it you're a student. We're taking on four at the most, and you'll require a National Insurance card. The work is paid for by the hour and there is accommodation if you can't travel. It's mainly routine work, potting plants and so forth, though you will be shown what to do and supervised till you do it properly.'

'Oh.' The student looked taken aback, then he recovered quickly. 'That's fine,' he agreed, 'if I've come to the right place. I was actually looking for Miss Hudson.'

'Hudson?'

Ruth's brows wrinkled, then cleared.

'Oh, Sarah. Did Sar … Miss Hudson recommend you to come and apply for the job?'

'Well … er … it's a long story, but she's certainly responsible for my being here.'

A grin appeared through the beard, and bright rather beady eyes surveyed her laughingly. For once Ruth felt discomfited, so she pulled a pad towards her.

'Name, please,' she said crisply.

'Clifford Ainslie.'

'Address?'

'You've just told me ... this address. I'm leaving my lodgings in Kendal today.'

'Oh!' Ruth drew a deep breath, then looked up with relief as Simon walked in.

'This is our first student, Mr Demaine,' she said, very formally. 'He requires accommodation. His name is...' She glanced at the pad ... 'Clifford Ainslie, and Sarah has recommended him.'

'I see.'

Simon's eyes swept over Clifford, trying to find the man under all the decoration, then giving up. If he knew Sarah...

'All right, then. You want to stay now?' he asked, 'or have you a bag to pick up?'

'Left it near the gate,' Clifford told him. 'Just a haversack. I travel light.'

'Well, there's the kitchen door, and if you go there, Sarah will see to you and show you

111

where you sleep. You realise that living in gives you a different salary scale?'

Ruth frowned, having forgotten to explain that, but she did so now, aware of Clifford's eyes on her full of amusement. She didn't know if she liked this young man.

But it was Mrs White who met Clifford at the kitchen door and took him up to the attic.

'I'm dealing wi' the students, young fellow,' she told him roundly. 'So you best mind your p's and q's. No noise and no mess, and no playing records and your guitars late at night. This is a lovely house, so see'n keep it that way.'

'It's better than the cave I was brought up in,' Clifford told her gravely. 'There wasn't much housework for my mother, just changing the rushes, but my bearskin wasn't half cold in winter.'

'Yes, well…' Mrs White was temporarily at a loss for words. 'Just mind what I tell you,' she said finally. 'You can have tea in the kitchen an hour from now.'

Clifford decided that the accommodation was to his liking, and that he had had a really good stroke of luck. It wasn't a bad place either, he thought, staring down from the dormer window. Quite a set-up! He had really only called to see Sarah, but a month or two being in the same house, with pay, wasn't such a bad idea. He'd been at a bit of a loss for a few weeks anyhow.

Sarah had been into Kendal on a quick errand. Her date with Simon to Windermere was coming up on Sunday and she had wanted a quick hair-do, and some new lipstick. Not, she supposed, that he would notice what she looked like, but she felt she needed confidence in herself, being faced with Simon's companionship for a whole day. What if he grew bored with her very quickly? Worse still, what if he'd forgotten? He hadn't mentioned the outing again to her, and it seemed to her it may have slipped his mind. Several times she had wanted to remind him, but the casual words which formed in her head proved very difficult to speak, and made her feel rather shy of him.

Now she hurried into the kitchen, putting away her other small purchases, her face still feeling slightly swollen from the dryer, and her exertion at getting back in time for tea.

'My, but you've lovely curls, luv,' said Mrs White admiringly. 'You'll have all the young students after you when they come.'

Sarah giggled. 'I've had enough of students at the moment, Mrs White,' she said, feeling that a date with Simon made her feel older, and gave her a new dignity.

'One's arrived,' said Mrs White baldly. 'Usual type with long hair and beard, though a few good meals down him and a bath or two won't go amiss.'

'Well, I'll leave him to you, Mrs White,' said Sarah. 'I'm so glad you're going to be here every day to help out. We're getting so busy now, and Mrs Demaine is out nearly all the time, and in any case, it's all rather tiring for her, so I don't like her having to help me if I can manage without her.'

'You're a good lass,' Mrs White approved. 'You've managed better than I'd have thought, looking at you. My girls would make two of you.'

Sarah wondered if she should apologise for her small size, but instead she quietly turned up the oven on her casserole, and hurried to set the table in the dining room.

When she returned to the kitchen she found the student sitting at the kitchen table, while Mrs White placed a dish of her own special brand of Lancashire hotpot in front of him.

'This looks good, Ma,' he told her.

'Less of the Ma,' said Mrs White severely. 'The name is Mrs White.'

'How do you do? Oh, hello, Sarah, there you are. I was wondering when you'd show up.'

Sarah was standing stock still, her face registering shock, complete disbelief, and hardly any pleasure at all. She had decided to forget Clifford since she was now living a much happier life without his influence.

Now here he was, large as life, and no doubt all ready to mess things up for her. It was so hard to resist Clifford's ideas, and he was very convincing at putting over his own particular point of view.

'Clifford Ainslie!' she gasped. 'What are *you* doing here?'

'Originally I came to see you,' he told her, eating his hotpot. 'Good stew, Mrs White. Then a ... young female who looked like the manageress of the Employment Exchange nabbed me and engaged me on the spot. I'm sweated student labour, no doubt overworked and underpaid. I start attacking the old greenfly in the morning.'

'But ... but how did you find me?' cried Sarah. 'Surely Aunt Muriel...'

'Was as close as an oyster,' Clifford assured her. 'Funny thing about your auntie, Sarah ... she doesn't really approve of me.' He turned to Mrs White. 'Can you imagine that, Mrs White? Her auntie hasn't a good word to say for me!'

'You leave Aunt Muriel alone,' said Sarah

angrily. 'I … I feel ashamed when I think of the way I used to take her for granted, so lay off her, Cliff.'

'Or out you go, my lad,' put in Mrs White warningly. 'I don't know what it's all about, but don't you go coming here and upsetting Miss Sarah. D'ye hear?'

Clifford held up his hands as though they were pointing a gun at his ribs.

'All right, all right,' he said. 'Two to one isn't fair, and two females to one male is least fair of all.'

'But how did you find me?' asked Sarah, still perplexed. 'Did you really go and see Aunt Muriel?'

'Sure I did,' said Clifford, reaching for some bread to mop his plate. 'At least, I went to see you, but there she was all on her tod, and she took a very poor view of it when I asked for your address. Anyway, she'd been writing you a letter and there it was, all ready to post on the hall table. Miss Sarah Hudson, c/o Demaine, Bonnygrass, Nr. Kendal, Westmorland.'

Clifford reeled it off parrot fashion, then he looked appealingly at Mrs White. 'That sure was good stew,' he told her, licking his lips.

'Good Lancashire hotpot,' she said proudly, and there was a softened note in her voice. Sarah felt ready to boil when Clifford winked at her.

'Don't give him any more, Mrs White,' she said indignantly. 'He's just being greedy.'

'Young boys *are* greedy,' said Mrs White, giving him a second helping. 'It's all right, Miss Sarah. He won't get round me. I'll keep an eye on him. I know his type all right, and he needn't think he's here for a holiday neither, for Mr Simon knows his type, too.'

'I knew it,' said Clifford, in mock despair. 'Sweated labour. What would they do without students?'

'You are no longer a student,' said Sarah severely.

'True. True.' This time Clifford's voice was rueful.

'Anyway, I've no time for gossip,' said Sarah. 'I've got to get a meal for Simon and Mrs Demaine.'

'Why can't Mrs White do that, and why aren't you in the office?' asked Clifford, curiously.

'Because Mrs White is not the house-keeper,' explained Sarah firmly. 'I am. Mrs White is helping out every day while the students are here, and we're extra busy.'

'But...' This time it was Clifford's turn to be bewildered. 'You mean you're here as ... as the maid?'

'The housekeeper,' said Sarah calmly, 'like I told you. Ruth Kirkham is the secretary, not me.'

For once Clifford was at a loss for words, then he drew a deep breath.

'If you ask me, it's time I was here,' he decided, 'to see what you've been letting yourself in for.'

'If you interfere,' cried Sarah furiously, 'I'll be mad! I've had enough of you and your ideas. Now I'm trying out my own.'

'They don't seem to be doing you much good, Sarah dear,' Clifford informed her.

'That's none of your business. Now, if you don't mind, *I've* got work to do.'

Swiftly she began to prepare the evening meal, conscious of Clifford watching her silently. Sarah felt rather guilty that she hadn't given him a warmer welcome, and oddly depressed that from now on things would be different for her at Bonnygrass.

Already her mind was clouding a little with confusion, and she wished Clifford hadn't come. Even the prospect of her date on Sunday failed to cheer her up. If only Aunt Muriel hadn't decided to write to her when she did!

'How nice that the young man is a friend of yours, dear,' said Mrs Demaine over tea. 'Are you sure he'll be comfortable enough in the attic bedrooms?'

'It's quite good enough for Clifford,' said Sarah firmly, while Simon eyed her curiously.

'Do you mean that young student we've just taken on? Is he a special friend of yours, Sarah?'

'Only a friend ... or he *was*,' she admitted, her cheeks scarlet, 'though...' she bit her lip, wondering how to put it... 'we haven't really seen each other for some time.'

'I see,' said Simon, his eyes considering her thoughtfully.

'You aunt must have given him your address,' went on Mrs Demaine happily.

'No, he ... he saw it on a letter,' Sarah said, her cheeks again flaming with colour.

'Enterprising chap,' grinned Simon, amused.

'Kendal was awfully busy today,' Sarah told them, rather desperately, to change the subject. 'I guess there must be lots of visitors to the Lake District.'

Hopefully she looked at Simon, wondering if that would jog his memory about Sunday. However, he merely agreed politely that it was a busy time for the Lakes.

Sarah scowled a little, thinking that she didn't really like Simon much anyway. He had no real interest in anyone but himself and Bonnygrass, unless, perhaps, it was Ruth. Was he going to marry Ruth? she wondered. She would make Simon an excellent wife and would be a real help to him in business. Simon was no fool and would no doubt consider all that when he married.

Sarah's eyes turned to Mrs Demaine. What would happen to her if Ruth became mistress of Bonnygrass? Somehow Sarah couldn't really see the two of them living happily together, and she had no idea how Mrs Demaine really felt about Ruth, whether she liked her or merely put up with her. Or whether she actually would like her for a daughter-in-law.

'You're very quiet, Sarah,' Mrs Demaine remarked, with a smile. 'I'm glad your young man, has come. It will be company for a young girl like you. Don't you think so, Simon?'

Simon scowled and mumbled a non-committal reply. It was obvious that he couldn't care less whether Sarah had young company or not.

She, however, was busy protesting to Mrs Demaine.

'He's not my young man!'

'Well, he must be interested, dear, or he wouldn't have followed you all this long way.'

Sarah nodded. The thought had been one which had already occurred to her, and it hadn't given her too much pleasure.

CHAPTER FOUR

On Saturday Clifford managed to corner Sarah, even though it was a very busy day.

'Relax, doll,' he told her. 'I want to talk to you.'

'I haven't time just now,' she said briskly, 'and don't call me doll. I don't like it.'

'Sorry, I'd forgotten you'd grown so particular. Shall I call you Miss Sarah?'

That made her laugh a little, and she softened towards him.

'Of course not, Cliff. Only I really am busy, and you should be, too. Our other two students don't start until Monday.'

'I'm giving the plants a rest,' Clifford explained. 'They begged for mercy, so I'm giving them and myself a break for a while, and fortifying myself with Mrs White's A.1. cocoa.'

'I can spare five minutes, no longer,' said Sarah firmly. 'What do you want?'

'I want to know where we can go to hit it up a little. It's time you began to give me some of your valuable attention. What about going dancing in Kendal?'

'Not tonight,' said Sarah hastily. 'I've too much to do.'

'If you say that again, I'll go starkers,' Clifford told her. 'All I've heard about since I met you again is work, work, work. You're making an absolute chair of yourself, Sarah, and letting everybody sit on you.'

'That's not true!' flashed Sarah. 'I work because I want to. You wouldn't understand that, Clifford.'

'Don't you have a day off?'

'Yes, tomorrow.'

'Thank God for that,' said Clifford, with relief. 'Now we're getting somewhere. Please, Sarah, will you come out with me tomorrow, and we could go a simple little picnic somewhere ... down to the Devil's Bridge at Kirkby Lonsdale, perhaps?'

She was shaking her head again. 'I've got a date, Clifford.'

'Who with?'

'It's none of your business.'

'Then I can only assume you're making it up to put me off. What's come over you, Sarah?'

Angry colour was again in her cheeks.

'I'm *not* making it up! If you want to know, I'm going to Windermere with Simon.'

'Well, well … how's that for a tale!'

Sarah looked round quickly, and tears of mortification swam into her eyes as Ruth walked in closely followed by Simon.

'You're quite entitled to turn down your young man, Sarah,' Ruth told her, quite gently. 'It's all in the game, but you really shouldn't use Simon as an excuse. After all, he *is* the owner of Bonnygrass, and our employer.'

Sarah didn't know what to say. She had never felt more embarrassed in her life. She glanced at Simon, who immediately stepped forward.

'I don't know what the fuss is about,' he said, mildly. 'Sarah does have a date with me tomorrow. I'm taking her to Windermere.'

'Oh!'

For once Ruth looked completely discomfited, and her poise was visibly shaken. She threw a look at Sarah, rather different from her usual friendly, casual, and rather patronising one. Then she smiled again, sweetly.

'How nice of you, Simon, to take Sarah. Of course she must see Lake Windermere … the other Lakes, too. I do hope you both have a delightful day.'

'Why don't you wish me a delightful day, too?' suggested Clifford. 'I want to see the Lakes, too, preferably in the company of a real stunning female like yourself. At least you could be, if you lost some of your starch and forgot the Good Works. So how about it, Ruthie? Want to keep me company tomorrow?'

Ruth was speechless, and Sarah wondered if she was imagining the sudden gleam of laughter in Simon's eyes. He had turned away too quickly for her to be sure.

'What are you doing here, Ainslie?' Ruth was asking icily. 'Why aren't you in the greenhouses potting? I understand that's what you were assigned to today.'

'Dehydration had set in,' Clifford told her informatively. 'I was dry, dear. This cocoa is saving my life.' He took a final swig at his mug. 'Ah well, since there is to be no love in my life, I must turn to my work, for therein lies the fulfilment for which I crave.'

He went out like a Victorian actor, and Ruth turned to Simon, her eyes still glittering.

'What an abominable young man,' she said. 'We ought to get rid of him. We'll likely have to turn down some good young men during the next few days.'

'He's a friend of Sarah's,' said Simon mildly. 'I expect he'll settle down.'

Ruth looked as though she didn't think much of that.

'Aren't you busy today, Sarah?' she asked sweetly.

'Very busy,' said Sarah equably. 'I imagine we all are.'

Picking up a tray, she made for the dining room. At least her potential date with Simon was now confirmed. But would he have remembered if he hadn't been reminded? she wondered, a small frown between her eyes. That was something she would never know.

Ruth hadn't liked it either. The glance she had flung at Sarah had certainly told her that. Now Sarah began to smile a little mischievously. She was woman enough to feel pleased!

Sunday was a beautiful warm June day, and Sarah decided to wear her cinnamon suit. Mrs Demaine had complimented her on her appearance as Simon went to get out the estate car.

'Sorry we've only got this for running around,' he apologised. 'I ought to have a car for taking out my girl-friends.'

'Oh.' Sarah felt rather discomfited,

wondering how many girl-friends he had.

'Maybe I'll manage one in a year or two,' Simon was saying conversationally, 'but I have to make do with this working model for now.'

They were taking the Windermere road out of Kendal, and Sarah began to forget her annoyance as she looked at the truly beautiful scenery. She had taken a lot of trouble with her appearance, but only Clifford had whistled loudly as he came down to the kitchen.

'So you really mean business, Sarah!' he had commented.

'I don't know what you mean,' she told him loftily.

'Oh, come, love, don't give me that. All done up to kill, when you're only going out with old Simon.'

'He's not old!' she flashed. 'Why don't you shut up, Cliff?'

'Sorry, darling,' he apologised. 'I hope he appreciates you.'

But obviously he didn't, thought Sarah,

then forgot to worry about her appearance as Lake Windermere hove in view.

'This is Windermere,' said Simon, as they drove into the lovely little town. 'Bowness and Ambleside are further on. Do you want to stay here a little while?'

'Yes, please,' said Sarah happily, and Simon, who sometimes took the lovely lakes and mountains for granted, began to see them afresh through Sarah's enchanted eyes.

'How good it is that people have this lovely place to come to,' she remarked, as they strolled along, and Simon took her arm.

'Yes, I suppose that's the proper way to look at it,' he told her, 'though maybe the people who live here get fed up with the constant cars and trippers.'

'Yes, but they have it all the time, so I don't think they'll grudge the little bit other people have from time to time.'

'Er – no, I suppose not,' agreed Simon, looking down at her dark curls. 'You look nice today, Sarah,' he told her, suddenly noticing it.

'Why, thank you, Simon.' She accepted the compliment with dignity.

'I think we'll have a jolly good tour of inspection, then we can have dinner at one of the hotels. That all right by you?'

'Perfect,' she assured him, and they began to enjoy themselves, as they returned to the estate car, and took the smooth road which skirted the Lakes. The names were enchanting to Sarah ... Thirlmere, Grasmere, Ullswater ... but she was tired when they finally drove back to Windermere for dinner.

'I've got scenic indigestion,' she confided to Simon, with a laugh. 'Every time we rounded a bend in the road, there was another perfect view for next year's calendar.'

He laughed.

'I know what you mean. Let's hope you haven't got the other kind of indigestion as well.'

'No, I've got a very good appetite,' she informed him, 'and don't dare tell me I need it, because of my cooking. Your mother thinks I'm improving every day, and she's bought me a marvellous new Continental cookbook, so look out for experiments.'

'I'll look forward to them,' Simon told her gallantly, then he looked thoughtfully into her glowing little face. Sarah was really a very pretty girl.

'You're quite happy here, then, Sarah?' he asked.

She nodded. 'I didn't think I would be, but I am, really. Bonnygrass feels more like home than anywhere since ... well, I suppose since Mother died ... though Aunt Muriel did give me a lovely home,' she added hastily. 'Maybe because it was a flat, and we were both out all day, she at work and me at school ... maybe that's what made it seem less like a home than Bonny-grass. Or maybe it's because Mrs Demaine is already a mother, and tends to mother me as well as you, Simon. She makes me feel sort of ... safe ... secure...'

Her voice trailed off and her eyes grew

solemn with thought.

Simon felt a sudden rush of feeling for her, realising that perhaps her emotional life had not been all that secure. Losing both her parents so young had been a sad experience for Sarah, yet there was no trace of self-pity in her. Even when she was being thoughtful over her reasons for feeling at home in Bonnygrass, she was matter-of-fact, and was now grinning at him as the waiter brought their order.

'This is going to taste specially good because I haven't cooked it,' she told him. 'I'm glad I'm starving, then I can enjoy it even more.'

Simon smiled and looked down at his own plate. Perhaps they'd been hard on young Sarah, he thought, with a pang of remorse and some other emotion he couldn't quite analyse, making her take on the responsibility for running Bonnygrass, even though his mother had kept a hawk's eye on her every step of the way, and had been ready to support her if ever she showed signs of strain.

He thought of the letters which had passed between his mother and Muriel Duff. Aunt Muriel, as he had always called her, had been really worried about Sarah, and had admitted to making a poor job of her final upbringing.

'I've obviously paid more attention to my work than to Sarah,' she had written. 'I thought that if she was clothed, fed, made comfortable and educated, I was doing everything possible for her, but I see now that I neglected the most important part ... Sarah herself!

'Now she takes everything for granted, and feels that the world owes her a living, and this young student she's so friendly with is, I feel sure, a bad influence. Now she can no longer carry on with her studies as the College Principal feels, quite rightly, that she won't benefit from them in her present attitude to life.

'I've no right to ask this of you, Constance, but if you could just take Sarah into your care for a few months ... there must be *something* for her to do at Bonnygrass ... then perhaps the change of environment will make her see life more clearly. She must learn to be a whole woman and stand on her own feet, but I feel my Sarah is all gold, and won't take much teaching.'

Simon thought of the letter now. It had been his idea to make Sarah do the housekeeping, and he had had to work hard on his mother to make her see his point of view. Mrs Demaine had thought that 'a nice little holiday,' away from Art College, with just a few errands, would soon do the trick.

'No!' he had said vehemently. 'She needs to be brought down to rock bottom and made to work. God knows we need someone to help, too.'

'Then let her show the customers round, dear,' his mother said.

'No!' cried Simon again, 'that's ridiculous. She'd have no idea and I don't intend to train her. *You* can do that very easily. No, she must take over the house and do the housekeeping. After all, if she married ... even if she married *me* she'd have to do that, wouldn't she?'

His mother's eyes had twinkled at him and he had grinned.

'Not that *that* is a very likely possibility,' he had continued, 'but you know what I mean, don't you?'

'Yes, dear,' Mrs Demaine said, then her eyes softened. 'I wonder what she's like now. She was such a lovely little girl, I used to envy Alice having her. I'd have liked a little girl, too, but all I got was a naughty boy.'

Simon had ruffled her hair in mock annoyance while she grinned at him teasingly. Luckily they had always been good friends and had been able to work together for Bonnygrass. Simon's eyes clouded a little. There were still some large rocks ahead before he had steered Bonnygrass out of trouble. Young Vause would be delighted to get him out. He could get a good price for the land if sold for re-development. Simon had seen him hanging around a few times, no doubt weighing it all up. When he approached him one day, Raymond Vause had merely smiled blandly and assured him that Simon couldn't help in any way. He had only come to see over Bonnygrass 'out of interest, my dear Demaine...'

'You aren't half quiet,' said Sarah, in a small voice, 'and you look as though you could murder me. If you feel you can't spare any more time, I don't mind going home now.'

'Sorry!'

Simon felt taken aback, then he grinned ruefully.

'I was just thinking worrying thoughts,' he told her.

'About Raymond Vause?'

'What do you know about...?' he bit his lip. 'Yes, about Raymond Vause.'

'But what could he do, Simon?'

'Nothing, I suppose, if I keep my nose clean and pay up on time. But I feel very vulnerable while he holds any sort of mort-gage on Bonnygrass. I must be constantly on the alert to make sure everything is going well.'

'Is there no way of shooting up your income so that you can make lots more money quickly?'

He said nothing for a while, then began to spoon brown sugar into his coffee.

'I'm developing a new strain in roses that was started by my father, actually. I hope to show one at Southport Flower Show later this year. That could bring in quite a lot.'

'Well, then, why worry so much?'

Simon's eyes were still serious.

'Flowers are rather delicate commodities, and can soon be destroyed. Just think if they got blight ... or if someone was careless or deliberately malicious and sprayed them with weed-killer. Anyone bent on mischief could soon wreak havoc among the gardens.'

'Mm ... yes, I see,' said Sarah, and now her eyes were worried, too. But surely no one at Bonnygrass would do such a thing, she thought, turning them all over in her mind, one by one. And Simon's watchdogs would soon bark if anyone tried to break in at night.

Then Simon was laughing and taking her hand.

'Anyway, why worry about things which may never happen?' he asked. 'Would you like anything more, or shall we go now?'

'Let's go now,' said Sarah happily, and they walked back to the car companionably.

As Simon took the road for Kendal, Sarah sighed happily beside him.

'It's been a lovely day,' she said. 'Thank you, Simon.'

'I'm glad you're happy here, Sarah,' he told her. 'I'd never have believed you'd settle down so well. You didn't regret coming when your young student friend turned up? He didn't make you homesick, then...?'

A thought struck Simon and he broke off abruptly, while Sarah assured him that Clifford hadn't unsettled her in the least.

'He isn't the young student who was involved in all that trouble with you, is he?' he asked sharply, and Sarah sat up abruptly.

'What do you mean?' she asked.

'The young man your aunt wrote about when she asked us to...' Simon broke off abruptly again, suddenly realising he was letting the cat out of the bag. Sarah had turned to him, her eyes sparkling dangerously.

'You mean ... you mean my aunt wrote to *you?*' she said furiously, 'not *you* to her? Was all this ... all this some sort of conspiracy?'

'Of course not!'

'Oh, but it was,' said Sarah, her voice suddenly quiet and silky. 'I'm beginning to see it all now. Keep Sarah busy, give her a job to keep her out of mischief...'

'Oh, for God's sake, Sarah!' cried Simon, his nerves already raw with worry which was constantly with him. 'Doesn't your common sense tell you we need you at Bonnygrass? Doesn't the fact that we *all* have to work all hours God sends tell you that we've no time to make jobs for anyone? There's already plenty to spare. Now, if you want to help pull Bonnygrass through, then get on with it. But if you want to chicken out, you can get on with that, too. I've no time to organise any kind of work therapy. Nor have I time for student demonstrations for easier hours and more allowances. You'll have to take it or leave it, as we all do, and you can tell your student friends so as well.'

'You talk of students as though they never did a day's work in their lives!' cried Sarah furiously. 'Well, I can tell you it just isn't true. Why, it's only...'

'A small minority!' finished Simon. 'I know, and I even admit they do have a grievance, but they suffer from layabouts getting in on the act, and they drag in the weak, who could probably otherwise benefit from their education, and leave quietly to go into a decent job, instead of getting thrown out with nothing. Don't forget, Sarah, I was a student myself once.'

'I'm glad you said "once",' she stormed, as

they neared Bonnygrass. 'It sounds as though it was a long time ago.'

The anger went out of Simon. It was true. He would soon be thirty. This girl was ten years younger, though it seemed a lifetime by the way life had dealt out the cards.

'Quite right, Sarah,' he said gently. 'Sorry I've spoilt a happy day.'

She felt choked with tears as she ran up to her room. It had been a lovely day, and he had spoiled it. So had Aunt Muriel! Just wait till Sarah wrote again.

It wasn't until later that she realised she hadn't answered Simon's question as to whether or not Clifford was the student who had gone to jail.

Oh well, it didn't matter … or did it?

CHAPTER FIVE

Clifford grinned at her next day when he came in with the other two students for a morning cup of cocoa, served by Mrs White. She buttered large pieces of teacake which they accepted with alacrity.

'Mrs White, you're my favourite girl,' Cilfford told her.

'We'll have no cheek,' she retorted, fixing him with beady bright eyes.

'And to think it was once Sarah! You've had your eye put out now, Sarah. You look tired today, too. What's wrong? Was the old boy too much for you, darling?'

'Shut up!' she told him furiously.

Cliff had a waspish tongue at times. She blushed now when she thought of the number of occasions she had laughed at his remarks, when they were aimed at other

145

people! Now she knew there was truth in the remarks about herself. She did feel tired, and hadn't slept well because her thoughts were beginning to confuse her. Simon confused her because she didn't know whether she liked him far too much, or not at all.

Now here was Clifford confusing her even more, calling Simon the old man. He was older than she, but she had never been conscious of this until Clifford kept rubbing it in. So now she looked at him rather sourly, but managed a smile for the other two young men who were busy drying their hands.

'I don't know your names,' she said. 'I'm Sarah Hudson, the housekeeper, and this is Mrs White who will be looking after you.'

'I've met them, luv,' Mrs White told her cheerfully. 'Took them up earlier to see their room.'

'Rick Markland and Michael Newby,' they introduced themselves.

'You can all have your cocoa here today,'

Mrs White told them, 'but tomorrow you go for it to the shed like Bobby Mather and Jem Johnson. Thomas will show you where.'

'I bet he will,' put in Clifford. 'Thomas takes a delight in showing us everything. He sure sees himself the trail boss.'

'He is the trail boss,' Sarah told him. 'Thomas won't stand your nonsense, nor will Jem. They know their jobs, and they love it, so you'd better be a help to them, Clifford, or you're out. He and Bobby Mather have to be out a lot working in people's gardens, but that doesn't mean he won't know what you're up to!'

'My, my,' he told her, 'that Simon's turning you into a nice little yes-woman. I thought Ruthie was the perfect specimen, but you're every bit as good. What is there about this place that makes everybody sweat it out as though their lives depended on it?'

'Maybe yours doesn't,' said Sarah hotly, 'but perhaps ours does. You'll be leaving here in another few weeks, but it's our livelihood now, Cliff, and everyone needs to work to make it a success, or...' She broke off, realising that her anger was leading her into indiscretion.

'Or...?' prompted Clifford.

'Or ... or the profits will be poor,' she finished lamely, but knew from the gleam in Clifford's eyes that he wasn't deceived. He'd be ferreting out the position with Raymond Vause as sure as eggs, she thought. Why on earth did she let her tongue run away with her? He had always managed to do that to her in the past, though it hadn't mattered then. She had thought she was in love with him, but now she only saw him as a rather annoying young man whose nature was more often bent on mischief and getting through life with the minimum effort on his own behalf.

Really, it would do Clifford good if Thomas made him work, as she had had to work in the house. It had helped her, taking on responsibility, and it might make a man of Clifford, too, though she still felt ruffled about the way it had all been done. It was annoying to think of Aunt Muriel having to write to Mrs Demaine to take Sarah off her hands. It hurt her pride to think about that exchange of letters. And how angry Aunt Muriel would be if she could see her sitting here talking to Clifford now!

'Anyway, you did me a good turn turning me down yesterday,' Clifford told her airily. 'I found myself being entertained in a very amusing place. With a very amusing companion, too.'

'That's good,' said Sarah, 'but really, Cliff, I don't want you here any more. I've got a lot to do.'

'Even if I tell you I was out with Ruthie? At her Youth Club, no less? I'm going to let her father reform me. I even went to church.'

Sarah was surprised, then saw that Clifford really was telling her the truth.

'Good for Ruth!' she applauded.

'Yes, it wasn't at all bad,' he mused. 'I thought I'd softened her up, too, but no. This morning she hands me the superior treatment and I'm back to menial status. Ah ... women!' sighed Clifford.

'If you don't get back to work,' said Mrs White, suddenly appearing at the kitchen door, 'Thomas will have your cards ready. The other two went back five minutes ago.'

'Clip me ball and chain back on again, then,' he requested. 'See you, Sarah.'

'Not if she sees you first,' Mrs White told him, then had a good laugh after he'd gone.

'He's a rascal, that one,' she told Sarah, 'but I can't help liking him.'

Sarah said nothing. She liked Clifford, too, at heart, but she didn't trust his behaviour too much.

The nurseries settled into a new routine, and from remarks made by Simon to his mother, Sarah gathered that the three students were pulling their weight quite well. No other boy had turned up looking for work, but Simon decided that they would manage very well with the labour they had now.

Sarah didn't see a great deal of the other workers while she was busy in the house, though occasionally she went in search of Jem Johnson if she needed more vegetables, and was greeted cheerfully by Thomas and Bobby Mather, who grinned and winked at her brashly, while he prepared plants which had been ordered.

'Get on wi' yer work, lad,' Jem growled at him. 'Don't let him give you cheek, Miss Sarah.'

'Oh, he isn't giving me cheek,' she told him, smiling. 'He's just a boy who fancies himself as a lady-killer.'

'Happen he is, happen not,' mumbled Jem again. 'Want some rhubarb, Miss Sarah?'

'Yes, please, Jem. I'm making a pie. Would you like me to do a small one for you?'

'That's very kind,' acknowledged Jem, 'but there's no need. Mrs Mather brought me a nice apple one yesterday. She's a nice woman ... needs a firm hand wi' young Bobby, though. They live in that group of cottages further on from me.'

'Oh, I see,' said Sarah. 'I'm glad you've got someone coming in now and again, Jem. Can I pop in and see you again one day?'

Jem hesitated, and the smile wavered on Sarah's lips. She didn't want to be a nuisance to the old man, yet she had enjoyed her last visit and thought he, too had liked her company. Her lovely embroidered picture was now hanging on her bedroom wall, and she felt very proud of it indeed.

'If I'd be in the way...' she began, but Jem cut her short.

'Come any time, Miss Sarah, any time,' he told her hurriedly. 'You're always welcome.'

'Thank you, Jem.'

Yet something troubled her on the way back to the house. She felt that Jem had something on his mind, and wondered what it could be. And in spite of being determined to accept young Bobby Mather for what he was, a rather impudent young boy, his manner was an irritation. She hated being ogled by a swaggering boy.

She walked back to the house, carrying her basket of vegetables and fruit, and paused to look at the monkey puzzle. Today the sun was shining and she could see its twisted, furry branches, enhanced by the brightness around it, and wondered why she didn't really care for it. Its long furry arms were being held out to her, and again Sarah found herself edging past it gingerly, then she walked smartly up to the kitchen door.

Her mind was in a bit of a jumble, but there was no time to ponder over her worries. In spite of her increasing efficiency, Bonnygrass was very demanding and Sarah began energetically to cut up the rhubarb.

A day or two later Mrs Demaine was late down to breakfast, and decided that she only wanted a cup of coffee.

'Are you feeling all right?' Sarah asked her anxiously, looking into the older woman's rather tired face.

'Quite all right. A bit fatigued, perhaps, my dear.'

Sarah wasn't satisfied and looked at

Simon who was putting down the morning paper, having no time to read more than the headlines. She motioned him out of the kitchen, and quietly shut the door.

'I don't think your mother's very well, Simon,' she said, in a whisper. 'Can you just look at her and see what you think? I'm going in to make fresh coffee.'

He nodded, his eyes as anxious as hers, and they went back into the kitchen where Mrs Demaine sat quietly at the formica-topped table, her pallor becoming increasingly noticeable.

'Are you all right, Mother?' asked Simon, pulling up a chair.

'Yes, I think so, dear.'

'Well, you don't look it,' said Simon bluntly. 'I think you ought to go back to bed.'

'But I can't,' wailed Mrs Demaine. 'Sarah can't look after me, and Ruth can't handle all the people who come, especially when you get called away as you do frequently.'

Sarah knew that Simon had to oversee

each new garden which was ordered, after which Thomas followed his instructions. The students were kept busy seeing that there were plenty of new plants laid out in pots for people to buy.

'I could help, I'm sure,' said Sarah eagerly, 'now that Mrs White is coming in every day. She finds it easy to look after the students, and can do a great deal more in the house.'

'Well...'

'If you don't think I'm capable of talking to your customers,' she told him, rather stiffly, 'I'll quite understand, but I think I know enough about the gardens now to be of help, and if you show me exactly what to do, I feel certain I can cope.'

Simon's worried expression softened.

'I'm quite sure you can do it, Sarah,' he said gently, 'but won't it be too much for you, organising the household as well?'

'It may not be smooth running for a day or two until I get used to a new routine, but that ought to sort itself out, too,' she said confidently.

Simon looked at his watch. 'I must go,' he said, and again his eyes were worried as he looked at his mother. 'Mrs White will help Sarah to get you to bed, Mother,' he said gently. 'I'll telephone the doctor from the office. I think he ought to have a look at you.'

'There's no need for that,' said Mrs Demaine, surprisingly firmly, 'and I'm not going to be stuck upstairs in bed, either. I do need a rest. I'm getting on in years for very energetic work, so it serves me right for thinking myself a young woman. I'll rest on the large couch in the drawing room, my dear. Sarah can bring me that lovely tartan car rug we bought in Fort William last year, and prop me up with cushions, and I shall enjoy a good rest.'

'Very well, I'll agree to that,' said Simon, 'but not to forgetting about the doctor. I mean, I'm going to get the doctor. I shan't have a moment's peace till he gives you a check-up.'

'But, Simon, I told you...'

'Yes, darling, I heard you. If you're only going on to the couch, I'll take you there. Sarah, know where to find the car rug?'

Sarah nodded and raced to get it, and collect a few soft cushions. Mrs White had come through to help, and although it was already a warm morning, Sarah switched on the big electric fire to warm up the room. She was glad Simon was sending for the doctor. Now and again she had worried about Mrs Demaine, noticing that the older woman looked rather tired and listless. She should have insisted on Simon doing something about it before this.

'Come round to the office when you can spare the time, so long as you feel Mrs White can cope,' he told her.

'Of course Mrs White can cope,' that lady told him roundly. 'I can run this place wi' me' hand tied behind me back!'

'I think you'll need both, Mrs White,' giggled Sarah, and was glad to see a brighter look on Mrs Demaine's face.

An hour later she went round to the office

where Ruth greeted her rather coolly.

'I'll really have to pop round and see dear Mrs Demaine,' she said, 'just as soon as I've dealt with the essential things.'

'She's sleeping at the moment,' Sarah told her.

'The doctor will be here when he can,' Simon told her. 'We'll go round with him and see what he has to say about her. You'll be able to cope for a short while, will you, Ruth? Unfortunately I've got an appointment to keep, but I shouldn't be too long.'

She hesitated, then nodded.

'Yes, of course,' she said crisply, and threw Sarah a cool glance.

'In the meantime, Sarah, I can show you, rather briefly, what you have to do,' Simon went on.

Again Ruth's eyebrows raised a little while Simon explained everything to Sarah. She listened carefully and made a few notes.

'If you get stuck, come to either myself or Ruth, of course,' he wound up. 'Think you can cope?'

'I think so.'

'I *hope* so,' Ruth told her. 'As company secretary I've already got a great deal of responsibility, but I've no doubt I'll be able to fit in time to help you.'

She sounded as though she believed Sarah would be needing it, and the younger girl's chin firmed. She was sure she had quite a good grasp of what Simon had told her, and would be able to carry out his instructions very well. She was fed up with Ruth thinking no one could do anything but her!

Sarah's first customers were a charming couple, Mr and Mrs Greenlaw, who had just moved to a new bungalow.

'We've come here to retire,' said Mrs Greenlaw with a smile. 'I must say I'm charmed with my new home, but the garden is non-existent so far.'

Sarah eyed them both as she conducted them towards the gardens.

'You look too young to retire,' she said, without thinking, then blushed scarlet. What a way to begin ... by making such personal remarks!

But Mrs Greenlaw was delighted with the natural honesty in her tone.

'Thank you, dear,' she smiled, 'and if I may say so, you look rather young to be an expert on gardens.'

'Oh, but I'm not,' Sarah assured her. 'I'm only showing you round because Mrs Demaine is ill, and if you want any specialised information, I'll have to take it down and Mr Demaine can tell you all about it.' She indicated her notebook. 'I'm really the housekeeper.'

Mrs Greenlaw's smile deepened. It was even more difficult to imagine this young girl with the slender figure and dark curls as the housekeeper.

'But I can show you round' she assured them both earnestly, and soon Mr and Mrs Greenlaw were admiring the gardens which were now at their best.

'Simon ... Mr Demaine ... can also design one to suit your requirements,' Sarah told them efficiently.

'Oh, but this is lovely,' said Mrs Greenlaw, stopping at one design. 'Don't you think so, Edward?'

'Very nice, my dear, though the choice must be yours. I wouldn't know the difference between a weed and a flower, not if you laid them down side by side. Florence will do the garden, and I'm going to write my memoirs: "Poison in my teacup".'

'Oh,' said Sarah, slightly taken aback.

'My husband was a chemist,' explained Mrs Greenlaw, her eyes twinkling.

'I see,' said Sarah, then went back to being businesslike.

'Of course we have extra plants and flowers over in those beds over there, and here's a brochure for you to choose from. There are still three more gardens to see, through this gate here.'

She conducted her customers round, feeling very competent and efficient as the Greenlaws admired everything they saw, though Mrs Greenlaw returned to her first choice.

'No, I can see this round my new home quite clearly,' she decided. 'I like the crescent-shaped flower beds, and I must have roses. Roses everywhere! Yes ... now could someone ... Mr Demaine? ... come out and let me know if he can make our wilderness into this garden, and how soon work could begin?'

'Certainly,' said Sarah, smiling. 'Mr Demaine will be delighted to call on you.'

'Then perhaps you could let me know when he'll be able to call?'

'He isn't in at the moment, but I could telephone...'

'It isn't fixed yet,' Mr Greenlaw put in. 'A small note should do the trick, then we'll know to stay in for him.'

'Of course,' said Sarah, writing carefully as she saw them to their car.

'Thank you, my dear, it's been very pleasant. You must come and see my new garden when it is finished.'

'I'd love to,' said Sarah, and almost danced back to the office where Ruth was on the telephone, and waited impatiently for her to finish.

'I've made a sale!' Sarah told her breathlessly, and Ruth looked at her with respect.

'Sure they're not "thinking about it"?' she asked. 'So many of them do first time, and we only get a small number who actually plump.'

'No, they want Simon to go and estimate for Number Three garden. It's for a brand new bungalow.'

'Good!' approved Ruth. 'Have we to telephone? I'd better write all this down in Simon's diary.'

'Write, not telephone, and let them know when Simon can go.'

'What's the address?' asked Ruth.

'You've got it ... haven't you?' asked Sarah, her heart suddenly sinking. 'Didn't you get it when you brought them to me? You said it was Mr and Mrs Greenlaw from Kendal.'

'No, you nit! Why should I take down the

address unless we make a sale? Don't tell me you've let them go, thinking Simon is coming to see them, and we don't know where to go!'

Sarah felt near to tears. That was just what had happened. She couldn't even reach the Greenlaws by telephone. Instead of finding a customer, she had probably lost a good one, because the Greenlaws might have come back often for fresh plants.

'I ... I'd better go and see if ... if Mrs Demaine is all right,' she told Ruth shakily. 'P ... perhaps I can think of some way to find the Greenlaws.'

'I hope so,' said Ruth, 'but I would have thought that getting people's address was elementary, Sarah.'

Sarah said nothing, but walked towards the house, her cheeks alive with colour. Simon, his estate car coming to a noisy halt, saw her and waved. Sarah didn't feel like waiting for him, but decided to do so, and face the music. The sooner, she decided, the better.

One look at her face told Simon that all was not well, and she told him what she had done as briefly and concisely as possible, suddenly glad she had got her oar in before Ruth.

'Pity,' said Simon, 'but maybe I can find out where they live by asking around. Don't worry, Sarah. Don't take it to heart, dear. We all make mistakes when we start a new job at first.'

'But I suggested myself for this one. I ... I thought I could do it, honestly I did.'

'And you can,' he assured her. 'The fact that you collected a very nice order proves that. Don't forget, we've still got the order. It's only the address we've neglected.'

'That's true,' said Sarah hopefully. 'Oh, Simon, I *do* hope it still works out all right!'

'So do I, so cheer up,' he told her, smiling, and Sarah's heart was suddenly doing funny things. Because now she knew that her very first sight of Simon had been the true one, for her. She loved him. He had been a bear to her at times, but now she saw how sweet and nice he could be when she needed it most, and she felt there was no one quite like him.

But he didn't love her. In fact, the only girl he seemed to care about was Ruth, who was no doubt much more suitable for him than Sarah.

'Penny for them,' said Simon, when he saw her gazing motionlessly out of the kitchen window, deep in thought.

'Oh, nothing,' she said guiltily. 'At least, I was wondering what to do about a quick lunch.'

'Fibber,' said Simon. 'I can always tell when you're bending the truth. You wet your lips and look everywhere but at me.'

'Oh,' said Sarah. 'Well, I can't tell you what I was thinking about. It was personal. And we *do* have to decide about lunch.'

'No need, luv,' said Mrs White cheerfully, as she came into the kitchen. 'Madam's having some chicken soup … very nourishing for her … and I've got meat and potato pie for you two.'

Sarah's eyes flew to Simon's doubtfully. He usually liked a good meal at this time, but nothing very heavy.

'Fine, Mrs White,' he told her heartily. 'Serve it up, then. Sarah and I are starving. She's worked very hard this morning.'

'She's a good lass,' said Mrs White. 'She's got a good head on her young shoulders and doesn't keep her brains in her feet.'

'If she did, there wouldn't be many of them,' laughed Simon, looking at her tiny feet.

'Well, it's nice of you, but I wish you wouldn't discuss me as if I weren't here.'

Sarah felt a tiny bit irritable. She had had a rather mixed morning, and now she felt battered emotionally. Almost immediately, however, she felt very contrite, and smiled apologetically.

'Sorry, Mrs White ... Simon ... I'm being disagreeable when I ought to be very grateful. To both of you,' she added, as an afterthought.

'That's all right, luv,' Mrs White told her.

'You'll feel better when you've got some of my good potato pie down you.'

'We'll go and see Mrs Demaine first,' said Sarah, 'only for a moment, of course, then I'm sure we'll both be very glad of our lunch.'

Mrs Demaine looked better. There was more colour in her face, and she had had a little nap before her bowl of soup.

'How are you managing, dear?' she asked Sarah.

'Not...'

'She's managing fine,' broke in Simon hastily. 'Got us a new customer this morning. Don't worry about us, Mother. It's you who matters most.'

'I feel much better,' she told him, 'and there was no need to ask Dr Travis to come.'

'The old gossip should have been here already,' said Simon. 'Even if I did tell him it wasn't an emergency. He must know I didn't send for him for nothing.'

'Now, Simon,' soothed his mother. 'You know how overworked he is these days. We must take his time. Now off you go and have lunch. Mrs White will have to attend to the young men soon. They'll be bringing in hearty appetites.' She turned to Sarah. 'Come and talk to me later, dear. I've been thinking quietly while I've been here, and I've got a few plans. I want to see what you think.'

'Very well,' said Sarah, and went off to eat her potato pie.

They were barely finished lunch when Dr Travis arrived, smelling of antiseptic, and wearing a rather harassed expression. He was a thin man, in his early forties, married with a young family.

'Sorry it couldn't be sooner,' he apologised to Simon.

'We understand,' said Sarah quickly. 'This way, doctor.'

She stayed with Mrs Demaine while Dr Travis examined her carefully.

'H'm, yes,' he said at length, and drew up a chair near the couch. 'Nothing too much wrong that a good rest won't cure. You've been overdoing it, Mrs Demaine.'

'I know,' she sighed. 'That's what I thought was wrong.'

The doctor gave Sarah precise instructions and wrote out a prescription for an iron tonic because he decided that Mrs Demaine was rather anaemic, then he turned to smile at Simon.

'I'll be along to see you one weekend, Demaine,' he said, picking up his bag. 'Need some plants for the garden, if I can find some way of shackling the children to allow them to grow. The plants, I mean.'

'I'll see what I can find that's hardy enough for you,' Simon promised.

'Good. Well, I'll look in again next week, but the secret is complete rest, Mrs Demaine. I'll leave you in good hands, I'm sure.'

He smiled at Sarah and picked up his hat while Simon went to show him out.

'Sit down, my dear,' said Mrs Demaine to Sarah. 'I want to talk to you.'

'Did you like doing my job?' asked Mrs Demaine, with a smile, and Sarah bit her lip before replying.

'I did at first,' she admitted, 'but I made an awful mistake, and I felt such a fool when Ruth found out. I forgot to ask for the customer's address.'

'Didn't Ruth give you the order form book?'

'No.'

'Then it was her mistake, too. If you'd had that, then you would automatically have filled in the name and address, so don't go blaming yourself entirely, my dear.'

Sarah began to feel better.

'I hope Simon finds them, nevertheless,' she said earnestly. 'I'll be so pleased if he does. I liked the Greenlaws.'

'Well, that makes me think you'll do very well, Sarah. It helps a lot if you can like your customers. So I suggest we swap jobs from now on.'

Sarah's eyes widened.

'Oh no, we can't do that,' she objected. 'You're not well enough to attend to the house.'

'No, I need a rest, of course, but that won't last very long. I've stopped before I became too exhausted. In fact, I'm probably a bit of a fraud, really, but that's just between ourselves.' Mrs Demaine's eyes twinkled. 'I've realised for a few weeks, though, that I must slow down, and I thought then that we could change places.'

'I still don't see how.'

'Mrs White's youngest daughter would be willing to come while we're busy. No doubt she'll make arrangements about having her children looked after. Besides, I've been running this house for years, so I think I'll be quite capable of taking it over again, and leave you free to show the customers round, and attend to their needs in the shop. Now, what do you say?'

Sarah's cheeks were pink. She would be delighted to swap jobs with Mrs Demaine. Not that she regretted the weeks of running

Bonnygrass. They had probably done her a world of good. But it would be fun to wear pretty clothes at work again, and she knew she would love meeting people and talking to them.

But what would Simon say? And Ruth? Ruth wouldn't be at all pleased, decided Sarah. She would have to keep her wits about her, and make no further mistakes, or Ruth would delight in being superior, and point out that mistake.

'What will Simon say?' she asked, at length. 'Won't it be up to him?'

'I've already had a word with Simon and he thinks we could give it a trial.'

Sarah's eyes shone, and her heart raced. So Simon didn't think her so bad after all!

'Then it's a deal,' she said, and impulsively reached over and kissed the older woman on the cheek.

'Thank you,' she said happily. 'I'll love it.'

Mrs Demaine nodded, her eyes resting thoughtfully on Sarah's small lively face.

'You're a nice child, Sarah,' she said at

length. 'Have you heard from your Aunt Muriel recently?'

'Yes,' said Sarah, a trifle shortly.

Her own last letter had been a bit stilted, written after she found out that Aunt Muriel had approached the Demaines to give her a job, instead of the other way round. That was still rankling.

'She's having a holiday next month,' she told Mrs Demaine.

'I know. I'm going to write to her to come and stay for a few days. She's going to advise Simon professionally, you know.'

Sarah was quiet, then suddenly the thought of seeing Aunt Muriel again was a delight to her. It would be fun to show her, too, that she was making a success of her new job.

'I do hope she comes,' she said fervently.

'She'll come, especially if you tell her you're longing to see her, too. As soon as the season ends, I would like you to take a good holiday yourself, Sarah. A breather will be good for you, and you can decide if this is really what you want to do with your life. Stay at Bonnygrass, I mean.'

'You … you mean you might not wish me to stay here permanently? That there won't be enough for me to do in the winter months?'

'I mean nothing of the kind. But you're a young girl with talent, and you yourself may find that this doesn't satisfy you, my dear.'

Sarah said nothing. She hadn't visualised a future where Bonnygrass didn't play a part. She had grown to love the place so much that she felt she belonged here, and it was her home. Was that only because she loved Simon, and deep down only wanted to be his wife?

But suppose Simon married someone else? Ruth, for instance. Then she would probably be rather unwelcome here and would have to think about making a new life for herself elsewhere. The future suddenly seemed an uncertain place, and her eyes grew shadowed.

'I … I haven't thought about it,' she said in

a low voice, and Mrs Demaine leaned back on her couch.

'Don't worry about it now, Sarah. We've got lots of the present to get through. I expect Simon and Ruth will wonder why I'm keeping you so long.'

'I'll go now if you're sure you don't need anything.'

'Nothing, dear. I'm very comfortable.'

As she left the room, Sarah's thoughts were still troubled. Mrs Demaine had given her morale quite a boost, then had counteracted that by showing her that the future was really vague and uncertain, and Sarah's delight had turned to depression. The telephone rang loudly as she was about to make for the office, and she remembered she hadn't switched it back through again from the lunch hour, so she hurried to answer it.

'Bonnygrass Nurseries.'

'Oh, hello. Is that the young lady I spoke to this morning? This is Mrs Greenlaw.'

'Mrs Greenlaw! Oh, how lovely,' cried

Sarah. 'I'm so glad you rang. I forgot to ask...'

'Our address, my dear. I know. Edward and I remembered later. Now, if you'd just like to take it down...'

Sarah was delighted to take it down, and returned to the office, with new confidence in her step. Perhaps things would work out well, after all.

CHAPTER SIX

Sarah settled into her job in remarkably short time, her confidence given a boost after her talk with Mrs Demaine. She got used to showing the customers round, and taking down their requirements in the order book, and assuring those who wished to think about it, then come back, that she would be pleased to show them round again, any time. A great many only came for plants and garden equipment from the shop.

Mrs Demaine grew stronger every day, especially after her iron tablets began to take effect, and soon Bonnygrass was in smooth running order again, with Mrs White's daughter helping out occasionally.

Sarah didn't see too much of the students, apart from Clifford, who often poked his head round the office door with the flimsiest of excuses. Sarah was surprised when Ruth didn't always squash him flat with a few well-chosen phrases, but contented herself by reminding him, mildly, that his work lay in a different direction.

'But think how much more energy I can put into it after a glimpse of two such delectable females.'

'Don't try being a man when you're still only a boy,' said Ruth, though there was no real sting behind the words.

'What do you mean, boy?' asked Clifford with exaggerated indignation. 'I'm just your age!'

In fact Ruth was four years older, but Sarah watched her colour with pleasure, and thought with some surprise that Ruth was no different from any other girl behind all that efficiency. Trust Clifford to get round her!

She caught him winking at her and felt suddenly angry. She couldn't honestly say she liked Ruth a lot, but she respected her and didn't want to see Clifford make a fool of her. Maybe she'd even like her a lot if she wasn't a bit jealous of her, thought Sarah, eyeing the older girl. Did Simon really love her? she wondered. Was he only waiting to get Bonnygrass on its feet before marrying Ruth?

'Sarah's gone to Dreamland again,' remarked Clifford, and she came out of her thoughts, startled.

'Are you still here?' she asked.

'Of course. I'm here on business, legitimate business. The old boy says have you ordered weedkiller and fertiliser, because the stock's going low in the shed.'

'Do you mean Mr Johnson?' asked Ruth pulling forward a notepad.

'Ar.'

'Then say so. I'll attend to it. Thank you, Clifford.'

He bowed out as though leaving the presence of royalty, and Sarah caught Ruth grinning as she made out the order.

'Don't take Clifford too lightly, Ruth,' she

warned. 'He makes fun and all that, but he can take things awfully seriously.'

'What sort of things?'

'Ideas ... beliefs ... that sort of thing.'

Sarah tried to remember examples. She didn't really want to discuss the old days at Art College when Clifford liked to take the law into his own hands.

'Really, Sarah, give me credit for some intelligence,' said Ruth, with a laugh, 'and isn't it commendable that a young man *should* have strong feelings about his own beliefs? It's much better than drifting along on the surface of life all the time, don't you think?'

Sarah said nothing. At least Clifford must be happy, at the moment, with his wages, food and accommodation. No doubt Simon would soon sack him if he didn't pull his weight, but Clifford was capable of backpedalling and encouraging others to do the same for some time before being found out, and losing Simon quite a lot in the way of work. Sarah resolved to have a quiet word with Jem just to make sure Clifford wasn't up to his old tricks.

He caught her as she left the office to go into the house.

'Where's Big Chief Bonnygrass today?' he asked.

'Out on business, of course, Cliff. Why?'

'Just wondered,' he said casually. 'No more big dates with him?'

Sarah flushed. Simon hadn't asked her out again, but she had decided that this was because they were both tired in the evenings, and liked to keep Mrs Demaine company.

'Still the big hero, Sarah?' asked Clifford softly. 'It's written all over you, love.'

'Oh, stop teasing, Cliff,' she said wearily.

'Then when's my date with you coming along, or have I to spend all my spare time organising games at Ruthie's Youth Club, and being a good influence on everyone?'

'You're not a good influence on me.'

'Then take me in hand and reform me.'

The kitchen door opened and Mrs White

poked her head through.

'Telephone for you, Miss Sarah. Miss Kirkham has rung it through from the office.'

Sarah was glad of the interruption. She didn't particularly want to go out with Clifford, even if he was always reminding her he had come a long way to be near her.

'I must go,' she said quickly.

'I'll ask you again,' he told her, turning along the path towards the gardens. 'You don't wriggle out of things so easily.'

Sarah hurried indoors and took the phone call, which was just an addition to one of the orders she had taken that day.

A few days later Sarah had the afternoon off, and went into Kendal to do some shopping and have her hair done. She arrived back home in time for the evening meal, and ran upstairs to wash and change before joining Mrs Demaine and Simon.

She had had a lovely afternoon. The small town was now very busy with holidaymakers, and she liked seeing the happy crowds and enjoying the carefree atmosphere. She had bought a pretty new summer dress in palest lemon which made her dark curls look very black. The dress suited her, she decided, trying it on in her bedroom, and on impulse she decided to keep it on. Simon never seemed to notice what she wore, but perhaps he would notice if she looked specially nice.

But both Simon and Mrs Demaine were in a very silent mood, and Sarah thought, a trifle crossly, that she had probably wasted her time dressing for him. Maybe he noticed Ruth's clothes, but he certainly didn't seem to notice hers!

Then she decided she was being silly, and she ought really to dress up for herself and no one else. She owed it to herself to take pains with her appearance. So she sat down at the table and beamed at both of them.

'Hasn't it been a lovely day?' she asked brightly.

Simon turned worried eyes to her and

185

Sarah forgot all about herself and her new dress.

'Is there anything wrong?' she asked, half fearfully.

'Do you remember Ruth ordering fertiliser and weedkiller a few days ago?' Simon asked tiredly.

'Yes, of course. Clifford came with a message from Jem Johnson.'

Simon nodded.

'Yes, all that was O.K. It was delivered yesterday and put in the shed. I don't suppose you saw anyone helping to put it in?'

'Only Thomas supervising where it was to go,' said Sarah. 'Doesn't he usually do that?'

Simon nodded.

'Thomas did supervise it. The weedkiller is always kept well away from the fertiliser, you see. The bags look very much alike. I wondered if anyone could have helped and accidentally put one of the bags in the wrong place. Was anyone else around later?'

'Everyone, I should think,' said Sarah.

'Everyone just comes and goes all over the place. I saw all the students, Bobby Mather and Jem ... and even myself, for that matter. One of the customers peered in the sheds going past, no doubt checking to see if we ran everything efficiently, or what sort of fertiliser we use. Anyway, what's it all about?'

Simon drummed his fingers on the table, and it was his mother who answered.

'One of the young students has put weedkiller instead of fertiliser on the flower beds. Luckily the mistake was discovered, but some very valuable plants have gone. The boy swears it was a mistake and it had been prepared for him from among the fertilisers. Jem showed him where it was, then he didn't think of checking up.'

Sarah's eyes were full of sympathy. She knew that Simon couldn't afford to have a single bud destroyed.

'Surely it was a mistake,' she said slowly. 'Surely it ... it couldn't have been done deliberately.'

Again Simon sighed.

'I'd like to think it was an accident,' he said, rather heavily, 'but it's one of the few small accidents recently. A hothouse door which was always kept closed was propped open … some pots have been knocked down as though by accident and the plants broken … little things, but they all add up.'

'I see,' said Sarah, her face going white.

'Of course anyone bent on real mischief will probably go for my new rose.'

'Oh, no!' cried Sarah. 'No, you mustn't let that happen.' The new rose was a beautiful bi-colour, lavender and pink, named Constance Demaine after Simon's mother. Sarah had been thrilled when Simon showed it to her, and told her that he intended to show it at the Flower Show. 'No one could be so cruel!'

Simon looked into her earnest face and a slow smile creased his own, while his eyes grew suddenly gentle.

'Let's hope everyone thinks so, Sarah darling,' he told her. 'I've asked Jem to give it extra protection when Thomas isn't around, though I don't know who'd be interested in giving me such a setback. It's bread and butter for the men, and the young students are just what they claim to be … boys earning themselves some money to help out with their grant. I presume your Clifford is also one of those?'

Clifford! Sarah's face paled. Surely it couldn't be Clifford? If something didn't please him, he usually protested verbally before taking the law into his own hands, and he had been remarkably satisfied with Bonnygrass, no doubt because his job here was only temporary.

'I can't see it being Clifford,' she said slowly.

'Nor Ruth, nor you, nor anyone,' said Simon. 'Only Raymond Vause, perhaps. You haven't seen him hanging around?'

'I haven't met him,' Sarah told him. 'I'm afraid I don't know him from Adam, but there's been no strangers around, only customers, and I expect if I took Mr Vause round under an assumed name, he'd have been taking a chance. Surely Ruth or Jem or some of the others would have recognised him.'

'Of course they would,' said Mrs Demaine. 'Anyway, it would be criminal to try to get Simon out using such underhand means, and surely Colonel Vause's cousin wouldn't be criminal.'

'I just know that it would suit him very well to have me out of here. He'd get a fine price for Bonnygrass if sold for re-development. He stands to make an excellent profit.'

'But he's wealthy, isn't he?' asked Sarah.

She had a vague idea in the back of her mind that someone had told her Raymond Vause had plenty of money.

'He'd never have enough,' said Simon despondently. 'Some people love wealth. Vause is one of them.'

'I think I shall go to bed early tonight,' said Mrs Demaine, rising from the table.

'I'll wash up,' offered Sarah. 'I expect Mrs

White has left by now.'

'We can both wash up,' volunteered Simon, 'then let's go for a walk, or a short run, maybe down to Kirkby Lonsdale to see the Devil's Bridge.'

'Oh, I'd like that,' said Sarah happily.

It was a lovely drive in the warm summer evening from Kendal to Kirkby Lonsdale. Sarah was glad, now, that she had decided to wear her new dress, and felt all the confidence of a young woman who knew she was looking her best. Simon stopped the estate car near the Devil's Bridge, and they leaned over it, gazing into the clear water of the Lune.

'There's good fishing in this river,' Simon remarked with a small sigh.

He had little time to spare for fishing these days.

'Come on,' he said, taking her arm. 'It's only a small town, but we can find something to eat, I'm sure.'

Sarah was charmed by the lovely main

street and attractive bow-fronted shop windows.

'It's a lovely little town,' she said. 'Oh … was Ruskin born here?'

Suddenly she had caught sight of the name being used by one of the shops. Simon looked down at her as he nodded.

'I thought you'd like it,' he said, with a smile.

They were both very quiet on the way home, Sarah because she had a lot to think about, and Simon, too, though he seemed to have shed some of his worries. It had been a peaceful evening, soothing to both of them. As Simon drew up the estate car in front of the house, she turned to smile at him and thank him for the evening.

'Goodnight, Simon,' she said shyly, and for an answer he leaned over and kissed her swiftly.

'Goodnight, Sarah.'

She got out of the car feeling a trifle shaky, while he drove round to the garage. As she was about to go into the house, she saw a movement at the attic bedroom window. It was easy to recognise Clifford as he stared down at her.

Sarah hesitated, wondering whether to acknowledge his presence, but after a moment Clifford moved away and the curtains swished across the window.

'I've been thinking, Simon,' said Sarah a few days later, 'can't you sell more flowers, now, direct to the public? Such a lot of cars pass and I'm sure people would stop and buy some.'

'I'm not sure that it would be worth sparing someone to serve customers near the gate,' said Simon doubtfully. 'Just leaving bunches of flowers in tubs isn't always successful.'

'No, I mean something rather more stylish,' Sarah explained. 'I mean ... I was trained to design boxes, you know. For example...'

She drew forward a pencil and paper, and drew out several boxes of varying designs.

'We could write "Bonnygrass Bouquets" across the front, like this, and I'm sure they'd catch on. I could get an estimate for you as to how much the boxes would cost. Lovely flowers, presented in a pretty box like this, would make ideal gifts. Don't you see, Simon?'

'See what?' asked Ruth, coming into the office, and Sarah bit her lip. She had hoped to sound Simon out before explaining her idea to Ruth, but now the other girl was looking at her designs curiously.

'It would cost a fortune and might bring in very little,' she told them. 'Not worth the gamble.'

'I don't think it would cost a fortune,' said Sarah. 'We can soon get an estimate, and we can try a few, surely.'

Simon was looking at her with new respect.

'These designs are rather clever, Sarah. You know, I do believe you've got an idea here … a darn good idea.'

'Well, don't say I didn't warn you,' said

Ruth, rather loftily, and Simon quirked an eyebrow at her. It was Ruth who was beginning to be irritable these days.

'Come now, Ruth, you know the outlay will be comparatively small, so long as the boxes don't cost too much. No, I think we ought to try it.'

Sarah was delighted, and sat down straight away to write to a Lancashire firm for estimates. She felt that her idea was a distinctive one, and might catch on very well.

'You feeling all right, Ruth?' she asked, suddenly noticing that the other girl looked rather pale and tired.

'Why shouldn't I be?' asked Ruth shortly, and glanced at Simon.

Sarah turned away, wondering if Ruth had guessed how she felt about Simon, and if it was beginning to bother her. But she needn't bother, thought Sarah. The morning after their visit to Kirkby Lonsdale he had again treated her coolly and casually, as though their night out had been a very ordinary one, no different from a business trip. If Sarah had hoped for a warmer feeling between them, she didn't get it. She had swallowed her disappointment, and her pride made her seem to forget that warm evening, and the quick kiss Simon had given her. He probably thought of her as a young sister, she thought dolefully.

The weather changed and for a few days it was wet and rather cold for the time of year. Sarah found that she had few people to show round, although she kept busy helping Ruth prepare flowers for wedding receptions. It was one line which Ruth usually kept for herself, having a special talent for flower arrangements.

Sarah also helped Mrs Demaine with some extra jobs in the house. The older woman was now looking much better, though she was inclined to be quieter these days, and Sarah caught Simon looking at his mother rather worriedly now and again.

'I don't think you need worry, Simon,' she

told him. 'I'm sure your mother is really quite strong.'

'I know. But she's a bit subdued, and that isn't like Mother. When is your Aunt Muriel coming to stay?'

'Next week,' she told him. 'Why?'

'Oh well, girls together, you know. I think she might do Mother a lot of good, and might set her mind at rest over our affairs. Mother worries far more than she need.'

'Are things becoming better for you again, Simon?' Sarah asked eagerly.

'Well, business hasn't been at all bad,' said Simon cautiously. 'We seem to have ridden those upsets O.K. We'll just have to keep our fingers crossed.'

'Wonderful!' said Sarah, and her eyes shone happily.

Simon squeezed her hand before walking over to his old car, and Sarah watched him go.

'All palsy-walsy,' said Clifford in her ear, and she jumped guiltily. 'Don't let Ruth see you or she'll bite you.'

'Cliff, what are you doing here?' asked Sarah, annoyed.

Living closely with the Demaines, her own slangy speech had almost vanished, and now Clifford's was inclined to grate on her. Had she really been like him? she wondered, looking at him more closely than usual.

He didn't look as carefree as usual, his face rather sullen and sulky, the eyes dull.

'A cat can look at a queen,' he defended, 'or should I be a nice devoted dog? I don't even get a pat on the head these days.'

She couldn't help laughing. She didn't know anyone who less resembled a devoted dog.

'You never accept a date from me, and I hardly see you,' Clifford complained, 'after me coming all those miles across country, walking and hitch-hiking, just so's I could see you again, and all I get is ignored.'

'I didn't ask you to come,' said Sarah, but there was a softening in her voice, and she couldn't help feeling a sympathy for him. He didn't look like his usual self at all.

'Aunt Muriel is coming next week, too,' she warned him. 'She'll probably throw a fit when she sees you here.'

'That's all I needed,' he said dolefully. 'Do I walk out now or wait till I get kicked out?'

Sarah considered.

'I wonder if she'll notice. I mean, she doesn't know you all that well, and I'm not going out of my way to point you out to her. Do you like it here, Cliff?'

'It suits me,' he told her flatly, 'though that young madam, Ruth, annoys me at times. She's so blooming lofty. She...'

He broke off and Sarah had a sudden insight into his ill temper. It wasn't Simon or herself who had caused it. It was Ruth. What had she said or done to him that was able to flatten him? Sarah wondered. She'd never accomplished that herself.

'How about it, Sarah?' he asked suddenly. 'Can't we go out one evening to the pictures?'

'Oh, all right,' she agreed. 'When?'

'Friday night,' said Clifford promptly. 'I

get paid then.'

'Done. But we go Dutch.'

'Please yourself.'

Sarah didn't particularly look forward to her date with Clifford. Mrs Demaine had some friends coming in, and remarked to Sarah that she would probably enjoy their company, as there would be some young people among them.

'Oh, dear, I've promised to go out already,' she said contritely. 'What a pity. You could probably have done with my help, too.'

'No, dear, you mustn't think that. We have no right to claim your free time, and of course, you must go out and enjoy yourself.'

'It's only with Clifford,' she told them, and Simon looked at her without expression. Did he feel there was no need to be jealous of Clifford, or didn't he care enough about her to be quite indifferent as to where she went, or with whom?

Sarah didn't know. Her feelings for Simon were beginning to bother her. At first she had been quite content just to love and admire him, but now she wanted something in return. Now she wanted him to love her.

Then Ruth would intrude into her thoughts, her arm linked companionably through Simon's, and her icy-cool beauty suddenly warm and soft. They had been friends for years, Sarah knew, and she would torture herself wondering just how they did feel about each other.

Then Sarah would begin to think about the future, and remember that Mrs Demaine had reminded her that she might want something different from Bonnygrass. But what? What could she do, and where could she go? She didn't really want to go back and live with Aunt Muriel. It wasn't fair to the older woman who was the type of person to be happier on her own. It was only now that Sarah could see how much she must have intruded into her aunt's life.

As she went to get ready for her date with Clifford, Sarah felt rather depressed, and a little bit frightened. What lay ahead of her? She had no real home and nobody, really, of her very own. Her sense of security at Bonnygrass was really a false one. She had been feeling like one of the family, but that wasn't true. Some day it would no longer be her home.

'I must say you look delighted to be coming out with me,' said Clifford sarcastically. 'Why didn't you dress in black and we could have gone to one of Ruth's father's funerals.'

'Oh, do shut up, Cliff,' she said irritably. 'I was … was feeling down about the future, that's all.'

'Why worry about the future?' he asked. 'The present's enough to be going on with. You're as bad as our Ruthie.' There was a hard note in his voice.

'Why? What's she said to you?'

'Oh, nothing.'

They were walking towards Kendal, and Sarah had to ask him to slow down.

'Aren't we waiting for a bus, Cliff?'

'No, we're not. I feel like walking, and so do you. We always used to walk, didn't we?'

'We did. Slow down, though. I'm puffed.'

Clifford slowed and apologised.

'She gets under my skin,' he said at length. 'Wants me to get a job … a *real* job, she says … use what training I've had in photography.'

'What's wrong with that?'

Clifford suddenly looked very young and sulky.

'Nine to five,' he said. 'House, mortgage, wife and kids. I'd be the same as everybody else. What kind of life is that for a man?'

'A good one … if you marry the right girl,' said Sarah mildly.

'You too!' he hooted, then turned to stare at her frankly. 'You've changed, Sarah. You used to feel as I do, that life shouldn't tie us down. That there should be more to living than just all this.'

He waved his hand as they passed along a neat suburb with well-kept houses, surrounded by neat gardens.

'Maybe there are other ways of living your life,' said Sarah slowly, 'but sooner or later,

I think, we feel we want our own home. I mean people have tried other sorts of society, but I haven't seen anything which seems to work. Have you?'

He walked on morosely.

'It isn't now that matters, when we're young and strong, but what about when we get old, or sick? Won't we feel we want to belong then?'

'Oh, don't give me that,' said Clifford. 'At our house we had Grandpa living with us for years, and he found fault with everything. He was always picking on me.'

'Horrible old people were probably equally horrible when they were young,' decided Sarah. 'Look at old Jem Johnson. He's old, but he's a pet. Anyone could put up with him.'

'Oh well, here's the pictures,' said Clifford. 'Two back stalls. And thanks for being so full of sympathy and understanding.'

Sarah enjoyed the film, and they decided to walk back home, fortified with a hamburger and a cup of coffee.

'For two pins I'd take you to the best hotel, order the best food, then wash up afterwards,' grumbled Clifford. 'I'm fed up ordering fish and chips. I want to start living a better life. Why should people like me have nothing, while the Demaines lord it over us with a tidy little place like Bonnygrass?'

'Because they're willing to work for it,' said Sarah angrily. 'The trouble with you, Cliff, is that you won't dig your own plot of ground. You want to do all the reaping, but none of the sowing. "Who'll help me eat it?" asked the little red hen.'

'How much ground can I buy taking crumby photographs?' he asked, then paused. 'I don't know, though ... others haven't done so badly by it....'

'There you are then,' said Sarah. 'It would be a start.'

'You get more like Ruthie every day,' he told her, disappointed, then laughed. 'I wonder if she'll be all mad at me for not turning up to her precious Youth Club tonight.'

'Was she expecting you?'

'I'll bet she was.'

'And you took me out instead! Honestly, Clifford, you'd no right to do that. I won't have you using me against Ruth.'

'I can see your eyes flashing in the moonlight,' said Clifford, as they neared the house, and turned her towards him, kissing her soundly.

But Clifford's kisses failed to move her. They only irritated her, thought Sarah, breaking away. He seemed very young and rather petulant as he stood gazing at her.

'I'm nothing to you now, Sarah, am I?' he asked quietly.

'Of course you are,' she denied. 'We've been friends for a very long time, Cliff. I don't love you, and I don't think you love me. I don't think you love anybody yet, except perhaps yourself. I think you're feeling rather sorry for yourself at the moment, but I still like you a lot, and I always think of you as a friend, even if I do get annoyed with you at times.'

'Thanks for the speech,' he told her. 'As to not loving anybody but myself, well…'

He glared at her and Sarah watched him go upstairs and pondered. Surely Clifford wasn't really in love with her? She hadn't thought so when he kissed her. Could it be Ruth he was beginning to love? They seemed so incompatible, though sometimes that was an attraction. Was that why Clifford was trying to struggle away from con-forming?

But Ruth also had Simon, thought Sarah, and couldn't help feeling a twinge of jealousy. Ruth already had so much … poise, dignity, brains and efficiency. It took Sarah all her time to get by.

She went into the kitchen for a glass of hot milk and found Simon already there, putting a pan on the stove.

'I'll do it,' she offered.

'Sure you aren't worn out by your night out?' he asked, and there was a faint edge to his voice.

'Why, no,' she said, taken aback. What had

made Simon so sour?

'Did your guests come?' she asked.

'Yes, they came and went. Mother is now in bed.'

So that was it! Simon obviously thought she should have stayed and helped Mrs Demaine, even if the older woman had told her she mustn't change her plans.

But Mrs Demaine had been right. She was entitled to her night off, and it was a bit of cheek on Simon's part to expect it of her.

'I'm sorry it tired her,' she said stiffly.

'It didn't. She loves having friends in. I trust you enjoyed yourself?'

Again Sarah blinked. Something had certainly put Simon in a rage, but she couldn't even guess what it could be.

'I did enjoy it,' she said slowly.

'Good. Goodnight, Sarah. I've locked up.'

'Goodnight, Simon ... is anything wrong?'

'What could be wrong?'

'I don't know. That's why I'm asking. I...'

But he had gone, and she was left to drink her milk which suddenly tasted rather sour.

She poured the rest away and went to bed, wondering what was wrong with everybody tonight.

CHAPTER SEVEN

On Monday Sarah was kept very busy helping to prepare for Aunt Muriel's arrival in between attending to visitors. They still had two days, but Mrs Demaine fussed a great deal over the guest bedroom, even though Sarah assured her that Aunt Muriel would be charmed with it, and that it looked beautiful.

'Such a view, too,' she said, looking out over the gardens where young Bobby Mather was sauntering about, and Jem Johnson was working among the roses. Clifford and the two students were no doubt in the greenhouses or potting shed, she decided, idly.

'That wallpaper is rather old-fashioned,' fretted Mrs Demaine. 'Muriel likes to keep up to date and faded pink flowers are bound to irritate her.'

'It's charming,' Sarah insisted. 'Do stop worrying. It's only Aunt Muriel, you know.'

'I know, dear, but it's rather a long time now since we last saw each other. Muriel was always so clever, too.'

'And probably she's just as frightened of you as you are of her.'

'Frightened...?' Mrs Demaine looked startled, then she relaxed and laughed. 'All right, Sarah, I'll stop worrying. Go down and ask Jem for a nice bunch of roses to put in this vase. I'm sure Muriel will appreciate them.'

Sarah went downstairs and out into the garden happily, almost colliding with Bobby who was making for the van with a box of potting plants.

'Oh ... sorry,' she said.

'It's O.K., Sarah,' he told her, grinning. 'You're in a big hurry today.'

'Yes, I'm very busy.'

'You're always busy, love.'

Sarah sighed, wishing Bobby wouldn't try

chatting her up every time he got his eye on her. He was still barring her way.

'Let me pass, please, Bobby. Thomas will be wanting you, anyway.'

'Let him,' said Bobby grandly. 'He doesn't own me. You know, if you made a date with me, I could take you to some real good-time places. I know my way around here better than some.'

'No, Bobby, I'm sorry. I've told you before.'

'Still stuck-up? I...'

'That's enough out o' you!'

Bobby swung round to see Jem glaring at him.

'Get on wi' yer work,' he growled. 'Let Miss Sarah attend to hers.'

'What business is it o' yours?' asked Bobby, colour rushing into his face. 'It seems to have escaped your notice that I'm not a lad at school any more. Just because I'm the youngest don't mean to say I don't get any older.'

'I'll treat you like a man when you learn to

behave like one,' Jem told him tartly, 'and that don't mean making yerself a nuisance to Miss Sarah.'

Bobby strode off towards the van with Jem glowering after him.

'Young rascal,' he growled, 'if it weren't that he'd a good mum … Oh well, I suppose he means no real harm. You give him a good set-down, Miss Sarah. That's what to do.'

'Best ignore it, Jem,' she told him, smiling a little. 'Bobby'll soon grow out of that phase. Can I have some roses for Mrs Demaine?'

'Of course. I'll get them now, or young Clifford will. He's working among the roses today.'

'Oh,' said Sarah.

She had just finished coping with Bobby, and had no wish to listen to Clifford's caustic tongue. However, Clifford was in a quiet mood as he snipped the lovely blooms, young buds, which would be perfect by Wednesday.

'Thank you,' said Sarah, delighted, their

fragrance delicate in her nostrils.

'Any time,' said Clifford magnanimously.

After lunch Mrs Demaine went to lie down for half an hour, and Sarah helped Mrs White to hang up some freshly laundered curtains. It seemed odd to think, now, that she had once considered this an impossible task, and felt, rather proudly, that there was little now about Bonnygrass which she couldn't tackle if she had to.

'I must have been awfully helpless when I came,' she remarked to Mrs White.

'You were just a young lass,' the older woman told her, 'like all the rest.'

Suddenly Simon strode in, his face white and his eyes blazing.

'Could I have a word with you, Sarah?' he asked, and led the way into the study.

Puzzled, she followed him, seeing that he was greatly upset.

'Did you go for roses this morning?' he asked, and she nodded.

'Your mother wanted some buds for Aunt

Muriel's room.'

'Who gave them to you?'

'Clifford.'

'Who else was in the gardens?'

'Why … Jem … the students … Bobby Mather … everybody, I should think, because Thomas was loading up the van, too.'

'So it could have been anybody,' said Simon, slowly, 'and nobody saw a thing.'

'What's wrong, Simon?' she asked fearfully, and he ran a hand through his hair.

'My new rose is ruined … the Constance Demaine. I won't be able to show it at the Flower Show. Someone has deliberately destroyed it. I … I'm afraid someone here is trying to … ruin me.'

'Oh, Simon!' whispered Sarah. 'Who could it be?'

'How should I know!' he shouted, then shook his head. 'I'm sorry, Sarah, I'm a bear to you at times, but this sort of thing … it's underhand. I don't mind a fight the same as any other man. In fact, there's a certain

216

exhilaration in fighting for Bonnygrass. In an odd sort of way, I enjoy it, and every payment I make off the mortgage gives me wonderful satisfaction. If I'd seen Raymond Vause hanging round here, I'd know where to look. It's just the sneaky sort of thing he would get up to.'

'Raymond Vause? But...'

'But it can't be Raymond, though someone among us is doing him a favour. The other things were small pinpricks, but losing that rose is a sad blow.'

Sarah sat down, her knees trembling.

'Who could it be, Sarah?'

She said nothing, hardly able to think clearly.

'Not Jem, or Thomas ... they've been with me for years. Young Bobby's a cheeky adolescent, but I've known him and his family all my life, too. He's no worse than the others were, and that sort of underhand sabotage is too subtle for him. His brains are in his physique.' Simon paused. 'The two young students are strangers, but I questioned them closely and I think they're innocent. They swear they've never even seen Vause. Clifford?'

Sarah was silent.

'Clifford?' asked Simon again.

'I don't know,' she whispered, 'but I don't think so. I don't think Clifford would do such a thing. If he disapproves of anything, he yells about it loudly. He's more open than the person who has done all the mischief.'

Simon's eyes were a trifle hard as he stared at her.

'I'll take your word for it,' he said heavily, 'and that leaves Ruth, yourself, myself, Mrs White and her daughter, and I think you can rule out my mother.'

'I think so, too,' said Sarah shakily. 'And yourself. And for what it's worth, I didn't do it, Simon.'

For the first time he smiled.

'I believe you, Sarah,' he told her simply. 'I can't imagine it would be Ruth, either. Ruth has been a wonderful help to me. She wouldn't destroy something she's worked so hard to build up.'

'And I doubt if the Whites would, either,' said Sarah dejectedly. She couldn't help a twinge of jealousy listening to Simon singing Ruth's praises.

Simon stood up.

'But I'll get to the bottom of it, if it's the last thing I do,' he said, with determination. 'I don't have my good hard work and loving care, not to mention my father's, destroyed by some stupid malicious person.'

Sarah looked at him and shivered, deciding that she wouldn't like to be the guilty party caught out by Simon. He could be gentle at times, but there was a hard core inside him. Perhaps it was that very hard core which made her fall in love with him, she thought, watching him stride away. It commanded her respect as well as her love.

She followed him out, slowly, looking at the wealth of flowers which swayed gently in the summer breezes. How colourful they all were!

Suddenly it seemed very important that the hand which destroyed so much beauty should be stopped before any further damage was done. The thought of all those lovely flowers lying blackened and twisted filled her with horror, and she felt the urgent need to help protect all this delicate life. Even the monkey puzzle was suddenly precious to her.

She stared at its twisted branches reaching out to her, and thought how much they resembled Bonnygrass at present. Which one of those branches twisting out towards her was really rotten inside, and ready to poison everything else?

Sarah walked on. It wasn't fair of her to think of the monkey puzzle like that. She'd got used to it now and really quite liked it and every one of its branches was completely healthy. Everything could be solved if only you faced up to it, and did something about it ... and the one uneasy spot in her heart was Clifford.

She had told Simon it wasn't Clifford's

thing, but there was no doubt he had been in an odd mood recently. Could he have tried to destroy Bonnygrass out of some sort of jealousy? Either because of Simon, personally, or because he owned these lovely gardens? Clifford knew that Simon was working on a narrow margin, and that the smallest piece of sabotage would be a setback. Destroying the new rose was a real blow to the heart.

Did he hate Simon because he was beginning to care for Ruth? Was that what was troubling him? Was it another blow to his ego, too, to know that Sarah no longer cared for him either?

There was only one way to find out with Clifford, decided Sarah. She must have it out with him. She must ask him, point blank, if he had anything at all to do with destroying that rose.

Clifford was looking quite cheerful when Sarah ran him to earth tidying one of the gardens.

'I've been looking for you everywhere,' she panted.

'I'm flattered,' he grinned. 'I didn't know I was in such demand.'

'There's no time for jokes, Cliff,' she said urgently. 'Did you know the new rose has been destroyed?'

He nodded soberly, and she looked him straight in the face.

'I have to know. I have to ask you, Cliff … did you do it?'

'That's a rotten thing to ask, Sarah,' he said, sudden rage colouring his face. 'Just like you, too. As soon as someone throws a spanner in the works, your tiny mind fixes on me. It must be Clifford. Or … or is it Ruthie who's accusing me?'

There was a hurt note in his voice, and Sarah felt angry with herself for asking. She knew, now, that Clifford hadn't done it. She knew, too, that she was still fond of him, and that he was falling in love with Ruth. It was all there, in his eyes, when he immediately wondered if she had doubted him.

'I'm sorry, Cliff,' said Sarah contritely. 'I had to know.'

'So that you can all comfort your precious Simon and tell him you've caught the naughty boy and thrown him out!' Clifford wiped his forehead, leaving it streaked with dirt. 'Is Ruthie hard on your heels to have a go at me, too?'

'Of course not. Nobody suspects you, Clifford, but I felt I had to know, and I could only ask you.'

'Go away, Sarah. I'm fed up being the dog with the bad name. And if Ruth tiptoes through these particular tulips, I'm going to bite her, too.'

Sarah turned away. She felt sorry for Cliff, and wondered if his love for Ruth was a permanent thing, or if it was like her own infatuation for him. She remembered how enslaved she had been at College, and even when they were parted, she had ached over him, then suddenly it had all gone, and Clifford had become an ordinary young man again, though someone still dear to her.

She would hate to see Ruth hurt him, but she doubted if he'd stand much of a chance with her while there was Simon.

'I guess Clifford and I are both out in the cold,' she told herself, as she walked moodily back to the house. But this time it was Sarah who would take longer to get over it.

The next day was Wednesday, and Sarah found herself looking forward excitedly to seeing Aunt Muriel again. It was only now she realised how much she had missed her aunt, and how deep was the bond between them. Sarah felt grown-up now, and that she would be meeting Aunt Muriel as an equal, and not as someone in authority over her.

The roses were perfect in her room as she looked round and gave it a final dust. Simon had spared time from his appointments to go and meet her at the station, and he had temporarily shed his worries as he hurried out to the estate car.

'Are you sure she likes salads best of all,

Sarah?' asked Mrs Demaine, as she fussed over the food. 'It doesn't seem very substantial after that journey.'

'The roast ham is substantial enough,' Sarah assured her, 'and Aunt Muriel doesn't each much after she's been travelling. She's got an awfully good figure, and she likes to take care of it.'

Mrs Demaine looked down at her own ample proportions.

'Oh dear! She's going to find me sadly gone to seed.'

Sarah grinned and suddenly kissed her.

'She's going to find you the sweet girl she used to know,' she said sincerely, and the older woman blushed with pleasure. 'If you must know, Aunt Muriel looks older than you.'

'I'm glad you came to us, Sarah,' Mrs Demaine told her. 'I wish...'

But Sarah never knew what she wished, for suddenly wheels crunched on the gravel outside, and she rushed after Mrs Demaine to the front door. Then she was in Aunt

Muriel's arms, smelling her expensive perfume, and trying to swallow the sudden lump in her throat when she saw tears in the older woman's eyes.

'Oh, Aunt Muriel, it's lovely to see you again!'

'And you, darling. And how different you look!' Muriel held her at arm's length. 'I don't know what it is, but I do think you've grown up.'

'I expect you think I look different, too, Muriel,' said Mrs Demaine, rather shakily.

'Of course you do, Constance. So do I. We're both older, my dear, but you're just as I've pictured you.'

Simon followed them in, after finding one of the students to help with the luggage.

Over tea, Sarah's eyes often strayed to Simon, seeing that he was making a fine effort to hide his worry, and help to entertain Aunt Muriel. Yet the loss of the rose, and the uncertainty of who was to blame, must be nagging constantly at his mind. If only she had the right to comfort

226

him, she thought longingly. He sometimes seemed to be so much alone...

Suddenly she caught Aunt Muriel's eyes on her, and there was a delighted look on her aunt's face.

'Well, your stay at Bonnygrass seems to have been very successful, dear,' Muriel said happily, and looked with equal delight on Simon.

It was easy to interpret her meaning, and Sarah shook her head hurriedly.

'No, no, Aunt Muriel, don't get the wrong ideas,' she said, without thinking. 'There's nothing like that between...'

She broke off, her cheeks scarlet, while Simon's expression was stony.

'I mean...'

'Your aunt means that you've grown prettier every day, my dear,' said Mrs Demaine, coming to the rescue.

'Oh,' said Sarah.

'Yes, of course,' said Aunt Muriel, recovering quickly.

It wasn't often she was caught off guard

and guilty of putting her foot in it. But she had been so delighted to see Sarah so obviously in love with Simon, and was certain that he must return that love, that she had made the comment involuntarily. It was what she had hoped for, ever since arranging for Sarah to come to Bonnygrass.

Now she looked at them a trifle bewildered, wondering if the excitement of her arrival had encouraged her into wishful thinking. At any rate, she had obviously put her foot in it, and she coloured a little with chagrin and disappointment. It was her dearest wish to see Sarah really happy with someone who suited, and in a charming place like Bonnygrass.

'I'd like to talk business with you when you've settled in,' Simon told her, after a pause.

'But of course, my dear,' said Muriel, turning to him with a smile.

'Yes,' said Simon, heavily, 'thought I rather think it's only going to be solved with sheer hard work ... and lots of much better luck.'

'I find that hard work often brings its own luck,' put in Muriel, and Simon smiled and shook his head.

'Not in this case,' he said quietly.

'But didn't you get the police?' Muriel Duff asked. 'Losing your rose was surely very serious and rather more than mere mischief.'

Simon ran a hand through his hair.

'I'd rather handle it by myself if I could. You see, it must be someone I know well ... someone working here. Besides, that sort of publicity is hardly welcome when I'm just getting Bonnygrass on its feet.'

'No, I can see that,' said Muriel thoughtfully. 'Does Raymond Vause know you're working on a narrow margin? I mean, providing you keep up your mortgage repayments, he can't have you out. Have you tackled him in any way at all?'

'Oh no,' said Simon. 'I've no proof Vause is behind this. It could be anyone ... someone getting at me, personally, even though I can't think what I've done to deserve it.'

'And you know everyone personally?'

'Nearly everyone. The students seem to be O.K. and swear they've never even heard of Vause. I believe them, too.'

'And the others are all workers who've been with you a long time?'

Simon nodded.

'I've taken Thomas and Jem into my confidence, and they're going to keep their eyes and ears open and try to protect the nurseries as far as possible. They'll check up on all possible sources of mischief. After all, it's their livelihood. Young Bobby's, too, to a certain extent, though he's young enough to start somewhere else, not like Jem. He's a bit slow, too, and perhaps wouldn't notice if something wasn't quite right.

'I've also got Ruth keeping a check on stocks, etc. She's got a fine grasp of everything and would soon notice anything amiss.'

'Yes, she seems a competent young lady,'

said Muriel musingly. 'And Sarah?'

Simon's expression didn't change, though he shot her a quick glance.

'We've been very glad of Sarah,' he said, quietly. 'She's helped Mother a great deal, as well as myself.'

'Yes, she ... she's settled down remarkably well,' Muriel smiled, 'though I can see signs of restlessness in her, too.'

Again she looked searchingly at Simon, but he was busy replacing all the papers in his files after Muriel had made the legal position quite clear to him, even though it was exactly as he had been told already. There were no loopholes which had been overlooked.

'Sarah's young,' he said flatly. 'She's bound to be restless. She's got talent, too. We're having some boxes made up to her design to help sell flowers direct to the public. I think her idea will take very well, and made a good source of income.'

'Good for Sarah. She'd have done so well if she hadn't got mixed up with that boy and his crowd. Their ideals were so much more important than work, but no doubt they know, now, that they can't live on ideals. I'm so thankful Sarah seems to have got over him, anyway. He just seemed to make trouble for her.'

'Well, she certainly pulls her weight here,' said Simon with a smile, 'and don't go lumping all students together. I was one myself not so many years ago, and our helpers here are always very good. I've no hesitation in finding them holiday jobs.'

'I'm glad to hear it,' Muriel told him. 'Well, if you can think of anything else, Simon, I'll be glad to talk to you again, but now I'd better go and find Constance.'

'We'll both go, Aunt Muriel,' Simon told her with a smile. 'I could do with a break, as I'm sure you can. Let's see if there's any coffee left for us.'

CHAPTER EIGHT

Sarah had begun to enjoy having Aunt Muriel beside her again. She had heard all her aunt's news about local people, and enjoyed listening while the two older ladies talked and laughed about their younger days.

'Honestly,' she said with a grin, 'how you two have the effrontery to pan the younger generation, I don't know. You were every bit as bad yourselves.'

'Oh, but I don't, dear,' Mrs Demaine assured her earnestly. 'I think you're fine young people with a lot more self-confidence than we had. Don't you think so, Muriel?'

'Too much at times,' said Muriel roundly, and shot a glance at Sarah, who refused to rise to the bait.

'I'll show you over the gardens after we've had coffee, if you like,' she volunteered, 'that is, if I'm not needed anywhere else.'

'I'll take over from you, Sarah,' Ruth told her.

She had just come in and had greeted everyone with a quiet 'good morning.' She wasn't really looking her usual self, thought Sarah, and she had been very late in coming round for her break. Unless, of course, she had been busy.

Simon had left ages ago to be in the office, and Sarah wondered if they had been having words, because Ruth was now looking rather ruffled, as though her normal air of serenity had been disturbed.

'Is everything all right, Ruth?' Sarah asked, going over to talk to her.

'But of course. What could be wrong?'

'I guess we're all a bit on edge these days. After the rose being spoiled, one wonders what to look for next.'

Ruth looked at her stonily. 'And everyone gets blamed,' she said flatly. 'Everyone starts to blame everyone else, don't they?'

'Who's blaming you?' asked Sarah, astonished.

'No one … yet. It's probably just a matter of time.'

'Don't be silly, dear,' said Mrs Demaine comfortably. 'Of course no one would dream of blaming you.'

'But people soon rush to blame others,' said Ruth again, her eyes on Sarah.

Surely Simon couldn't have blamed Ruth, thought Sarah. He always considered her above suspicion of any kind. So far as she knew, he had blamed no one yet. In fact, it was only she, Sarah, who had been suspicious of anyone, and had soon cleared that up by doing something about it. She had gone to Clifford straight away … Clifford!

The colour rushed to Sarah's face. Was that it? Had Clifford tackled Ruth, and now here was Ruth furious with her because of it?

Sarah looked round uneasily. She couldn't bring it all out into the open, not with Aunt Muriel and Mrs Demaine sitting there.

Ruth was looking at her rather contemptuously, and she coloured even more furiously. Trust Clifford to give it all away, though maybe he couldn't be blamed for that. It was her fault for rushing to him straight away, but she had to be sure for her own peace of mind. It would have been terrible to think that she had even been the indirect cause of ruining the rose, and she had been indirectly responsible for bringing Clifford here.

'Who will be next, Sarah?' asked Ruth quietly, putting down her cup.

'N ... nobody ... I ... I don't know,' she stammered.

She felt at a horrible disadvantage, and as though she had lost her self-respect, and this made her feel small and mean. She had been feeling capable of holding her own with Ruth for some time, but now she felt like crawling into a hole.

'Thank you for the coffee, Mrs Demaine. See you all later. Hope you like the gardens, Miss Duff.'

Ruth smiled pleasantly at Aunt Muriel, then swept out towards the office.

'She certainly seems a smart young woman,' remarked Aunt Muriel after the door closed.

'Ruth keeps us all in order,' Mrs Demaine told her, then sighed rather tiredly.

The gardens looked beautiful when Sarah escorted Aunt Muriel out of the kitchen door and along the small path past the monkey puzzle. She looked around, slightly uneasily, for Clifford and was glad there was no sign of him.

Aunt Muriel had already seen him, briefly, but he had been with the other two students, and she had lumped all three together without recognising Cliff. Sarah had sighed thankfully. Until then she had been putting Aunt Muriel's reaction to finding him here right at the back of her mind, otherwise she would have worried herself into doing something stupid. Now she decided that if he remained quite calm and cool, Aunt Muriel wouldn't notice Clifford in particular, and everything would be all right. Obviously he liked being here at Bonnygrass or he would have left after the first couple of days, and Sarah had no wish to lose him his job ... or her own...!

Now she was delighted to see her aunt was far too interested in the lovely gardens to look too closely at the people working around.

'Oh, this is lovely!' she exclaimed, as she came to garden number three.

'Yes, it's one of the most popular,' Sarah told her knowledgeably, and went into technical details. 'It's ideal for the smaller home, and makes a small garden look much more spacious,' she finished, and Aunt Muriel grinned.

'It's a good job I live in a flat, Sarah dear, or you'd no doubt be selling it to me.'

Sarah coloured.

'Sorry, Aunt Muriel ... I get so used to showing people round, and answering their queries, that I've got it off pat now.'

'I'm delighted to hear it,' Aunt Muriel told her. 'Now that you've had these few months here, have you managed to sort out your thoughts about the future? I mean, one reason why I wanted you to take this job was so that you could stand back a little and take a good look at your life. So that when Constance said she needed…'

'I know about the letters, Aunt Muriel,' said Sarah quietly.

This time it was her aunt's turn to blush. 'You … you know…?'

'Yes. I got it out of Simon. I know you asked the Demaines to take me.'

'Oh!'

Muriel Duff swung her slender legs as they walked to the next garden, and glanced sideways at her niece. Sarah was certainly no child now, and she'd have to remember that.

'Are you very angry with me, dear?' she asked, rather timidly for her.

'No, I'm not angry at all. In fact, it was only after I'd come here that I realised what a trial I must have been to you, and I'm sorry for the time I wasted.'

'Oh, darling, you were never that. You were just a normal child, but I had to get you away from ... from poor influences.'

'I know.'

'But do you want to make this your career, Sarah? Or do you want to go back to designing?'

Sarah bit her lip.

'Best of all I'd like to see you in your own home,' said Aunt Muriel, but Sarah avoided her eyes and shook her head.

'There's no prospect of that,' she said, with a small laugh. 'I ... I haven't really made any plans yet. It's still the busy season and will be for at least another ten weeks. Mrs Demaine isn't terribly strong, and Simon can't afford a big staff, so I can't leave yet.'

Muriel looked at her downcast face, wondering whether her first suspicions were correct. Was Sarah in love with Simon Demaine? Of course there was that young woman, Ruth, who was undoubtedly attractive and seemed more than usually friendly with Simon … or there might even be someone else living in the neighbourhood.

Of course, there was Simon's financial position. He would have to economise for some time yet before he had Bonnygrass in the clear.

'You'd better come back home to Humberton at the end of the season, Sarah,' she decided.

That young man had not come back again to ask after Sarah, and in any case, she doubted if this new Sarah would have anything to do with him. She would be able to see through that young … Clifford? … now and would have more sense than be influenced by him.

'I … I don't know, Aunt Muriel.'

'If you aren't going to marry, you must train for a proper career,' said Muriel firmly. 'My father decided that I should do that, and I've always been grateful for his foresight. I've led a very full and satisfying life, and I've loved my work. No doubt I should have had the same satisfaction and happiness from caring for a husband and children, but I never had the opportunity, so just think where I might have been if my parents had decided I needed no training because I was a girl, and would marry. I'd have lived a very poor life. Mind you, you're prettier than I was, just as your mother was prettier,' declared Muriel honestly. 'It's more likely that you will marry, as she did, but I don't think a good training is ever wasted. Think about it, darling, and let me know. I can afford it, Sarah.'

The girl felt a rush of affection for the older woman. She appreciated that Aunt Muriel was trying to do her best for her, and felt quite touched by it. Besides, if Simon did get engaged to Ruth, she would want to leave, and she would be very glad of Aunt Muriel to comfort her.

'Thank you, Aunt Muriel,' she said huskily. 'I'll be glad to take you up on that.

I ... I haven't very much saved, really, because Simon can't afford large salaries, and ... and I needed some new clothes and to go to the hairdresser's...'

'Don't worry about that. When you're a fabulous designer, you can make a fortune for both of us.'

Aunt Muriel grinned and took her arm as they walked round the last of the gardens and made for the greenhouses.

Suddenly the door flew open and Clifford strode out, pausing to stare at Sarah and Aunt Muriel.

'Hello, Sarah,' he said, with a grin. 'Hello, Miss Duff. Did you like the gardens ... all the pretty flowers?'

Sarah could have kicked him, as she glanced quickly at her aunt who looked as though she had been hung up at a dropping well.

'You ... you're that boy,' she said at length, 'You ... you're...'

'Clifford Ainslie. At your service, ma'am.'

'What are *you* doing here? Sarah! How

dare you bring this young man with you?'

'I *didn't* bring him with me!'

'Invite him to come here, then. Otherwise how would he be here? Does Simon know who he is? Does he know that this is the young man who could well have landed you in jail...?'

'You'd have been good at your job if you'd let that happen!' broke in Clifford, and Aunt Muriel's looks were ready to slay him.

'And who landed in jail himself!'

'What for?'

Sarah spun round to see Ruth looking at the three of them.

'Were you in jail, Clifford?' she asked.

'Yes, I was,' he told her flatly. 'I was criminal enough to create a disturbance and bop a policeman in the heat of the moment. I got an example made of me.'

'Well, you've no business to go latching on to my niece,' cried Aunt Muriel. 'Why can't you leave her alone?'

'He's only here for the summer vacation,' said Sarah desperately. 'Do stop, Aunt

Muriel, and give Cliff a chance to explain. He's only working here as one of the students ... nothing else ... and I think you ought to come back to the house now and let Clifford get on with his work.'

'So long as it *is* work, not mischief,' Aunt Muriel returned. 'I don't remember that he showed himself particularly fond of work for its own sake in the past.'

For once Ruth was having little to say as she stared, perplexed, from Aunt Muriel back to Clifford who was preparing to go into one of his clowning acts.

'Come on, Aunt Muriel,' Sarah said, taking her arm firmly.

'There was a phone call for you. Those box people. You've to ring back as soon as possible,' Ruth told her quickly. 'I came over to find you.'

'All right. Thanks, Ruth.'

Sarah was glad of the respite as she left Aunt Muriel at the kitchen door, and went to take the phone call. It was quarter of an hour later before she made her way back to the house, hoping that Aunt Muriel would have cooled down.

That was wishful thinking, however. Aunt Muriel had been furiously angry when she found Clifford installed at Bonnygrass. She had been relieved and happy that Sarah seemed to be over her attachment to the young man, and was now leading a happy life. To find that, far from being in the past, Clifford was now, in fact, happily working away here beside her, and even living in the same house, was a big disappointment and shock. And to think that Sarah had deviously engineered his presence into Bonnygrass without telling Simon or Constance who the young man was only adding fuel to the fire. Muriel Duff couldn't remember ever having been so angry.

'You mean ... this is the student you wrote to us about?' asked Simon, perplexed. 'The one who got Sarah fired from College?'

'That's exactly what I mean.'

'But I asked her...'

Simon wrinkled his brows. He had asked

Sarah if Clifford Ainslie was that boy, and she had said … she had said… No, he couldn't remember *what* Sarah had said. Surely she hadn't lied to him…

'He was a trouble-maker,' said Muriel, beginning to feel the tears not far away. The more she thought about it, the more upset she became. 'He is one of those people who want to alter our whole social structure. I … I suppose if he wanted Sarah, he … he wouldn't think it necessary for them to marry. He'd just want them to set up house together. Be free! That sort of thing.'

'Oh, Muriel, no! No, dear, I'm quite sure you're wrong,' Mrs Demaine quavered a little. 'I don't think he's that sort of boy, and Sarah certainly isn't that sort of girl. Though, of course, she's very generous, and very loving.'

'That's what I mean,' flashed Muriel. 'That's what I was protecting her from. Sarah could easily be led into muddled thinking by a boy with distorted ideas. You do see that, don't you, Constance? Simon?

247

It disappoints and shocks me greatly to find him here. I mean, it shows she must have been in touch with him, and put it to him to apply for one of the students' jobs. And he isn't even a student. Not now.'

Aunt Muriel was using every argument which occurred to her in her chagrin. How dared Sarah do such a thing! So Bonnygrass hadn't really helped at all!

'You need look no further for your mischief-maker, Simon,' she said, playing her final card.

Simon's eyes darkened with shock.

'You mean you think...?'

'But of course. Who else?'

'But why? What could his motive be?'

Aunt Muriel spread out her hands.

'Yes, what could his motive be, Aunt Muriel?' asked Sarah quietly, as she walked into the room. 'I couldn't help overhearing. Why should Clifford want to do all those horrible things to Bonnygrass?'

'You tell us,' said Ruth, her eyes gleaming at Sarah. 'You were quick enough to run accusing him yourself!'

'Oh!' cried Muriel, in triumph. 'There you are, then. If Sarah thought he had done it, you can bet your boots he *did* do it. She'd put him *last* on her list of suspects.'

'That's not true!' cried Sarah. 'I mean, I don't think he did it at all.'

'Then why did you accuse him?' asked Ruth.

'I didn't! I didn't! I only asked him to make sure in my own mind. I mean ... I'm responsible for him being here...'

'There you are,' cried Muriel again, and Simon's face grew cold and hard.

'You mean, you invited your young man here without being open and above-board, Sarah? Surely you must know there was no need for that. If you'd asked him to apply normally, and said he was a special friend...'

'It wasn't like that at all!' cried Sarah. 'I *didn't* know he was coming. Oh, dear...'

She looked round, her eyes stormy with tears and rage. She was becoming very confused and felt powerless to explain all the facts to them. What was the use, anyway? she thought tiredly. Simon obviously believed the worst, and it would be practically impossible to make him believe Clifford didn't mean anything to her now. Besides, he wouldn't really care anyway.

'Clifford didn't harm the rose,' she said stubbornly, in a low voice. 'Nor did he destroy any plants with weedkiller, or leave hothouse doors open. He did none of those things.'

But even in her own ears, it sounded as though she was just defending him blindly.

'I'm afraid he will have to go,' Simon said heavily. 'I'm sorry, but I can't take chances. Not if there's even the slightest doubt. Ainslie will have to leave today.'

'But that's not fair!'

Simon's face was very white, his eyes glittering black.

'I ought to ask you to go, too,' he told her tightly, 'but instead I am insisting that you stay. The loss of that rose means a great deal of leeway has to be made up, and we can't afford any further loss in man-power. You're needed here, Sarah, and you'd better work hard and help to make up the deficiency caused by all this upset since you're responsible for the young man being here.'

Sarah had been about to throw in her lot with Clifford. If he got fired, unjustly, she was going, too, she decided grandly. Now she realised that the bravest thing to do would be to stay. No one was going to accuse her of helping to ruin Bonnygrass, and if Clifford wasn't guilty, the best way to find out the real truth would be by staying.

'Don't worry, Simon,' she flung at him. 'You'll get your pound of flesh out of me. You won't be out of pocket.'

Ruth was still standing, her face as white as Simon's.

'Get his cards and his money made up, Ruth,' Simon commanded. 'In lieu of notice, and if that's Thomas and young Bobby back, tell Bobby to find Ainslie for me. I'll see him alone in my office.'

For once Ruth didn't answer him, but her mouth tightened and she stalked out of the room. A moment later Simon followed.

When they had gone, it was very quiet and the three that were left looked at each other miserably. There was cold defiance in Sarah's eyes, and the rage was gradually dying out of Aunt Muriel. She suddenly looked rather old and tired.

'How could you, Sarah?' she asked shakily.

'You ask me that?' Sarah turned on her. 'Didn't it occur to you for one moment to ask for my side of the story? You've leapt to conclusion after conclusion. You've assumed that I invited Cliff here, when it was your own doing … by leaving a letter to me around with my new address, so easy to read and remember!'

Aunt Muriel's face had gone very white, then the blood rush into it.

'You mean…?'

'Oh, what does it matter?' asked Sarah tiredly. 'You're all alike. You think you know it all. We're the irresponsible ones who do stupid things and don't stop to think. And even if I *had* asked Clifford to come, I wouldn't be ashamed. He's worked well for Simon, and now, thanks to you, he gets the sack through no fault of his own, that's what!'

Swiftly she rose and ran out of the room, up to her bedroom, where she flung herself, weeping, on to the bed. How dared Aunt Muriel behave in this way! Why did she have to fly off the handle as soon as she set eyes on Cliff? And why couldn't they get at the facts quietly and reasonably? Simon had been so quick to fasten the blame on her, too. She clasped her hands fiercely, hating him in her anger.

She decided to see Clifford before he went. If he'd wanted her with him, she might just have gone, too, but now she was committed to working harder than ever. Besides, she knew instinctively that Clifford wouldn't want her along, and she was imprisoned by lack of money. She would hardly have enough to last the week.

'I'll show them,' she said fiercely. 'I'll find out who's *really* doing that damage, then Simon can go down on his bended knees, that's what!'

Suddenly she felt better, with the determination to do something about it before her. She would show them who was right, and she would insist on a proper apology, both to herself and Clifford.

Downstairs Muriel was looking forlornly at Constance Demaine.

'I'm a fool, Constance,' she said. 'When it comes to handling Sarah, I haven't a brain in my head. If there's a right way and a wrong one, I choose the wrong.'

'It isn't easy, Muriel, especially at her age, when it's so easy to hurt her tender young feelings. I know. Simon was a tender plant, too, until he had to be tough. That was when he found he had a hard struggle ahead for Bonnygrass, but was determined to succeed. Life's knocks can soon make them into properly balanced people.'

'I suppose so,' said Muriel dolefully. 'What

do you think about that boy … Clifford?'

'He seems a nice enough boy to me,' said Mrs Demaine, 'a little brash, perhaps, but in no way malicious. I … I don't really think he is our culprit.'

'Then…'

'I think it's too late to keep him on, but I've warned Simon not to accuse anyone without proof, and if I may say so, Muriel, I'm surprised at you doing so in your profession.'

Muriel had the grace to colour deeply.

'Haven't you heard, Constance? Cobblers' children often run bare-footed…'

'Maybe so, but we must see that Clifford Ainslie will not be saddled with such an accusation and given the sack because he's under suspicion. That would give him a big thing to grouse about … a chip on the shoulder, as they say … and he would be quite justified in making Simon pay dearly if he's been wrongly accused … as I think he is. I won't blame the young man for being very angry indeed.'

'Oh, dear, it's really all my fault!'

'Perhaps it's just the fault of circumstances, Muriel dear. Don't distress yourself. This might make a man of young Ainslie. He needs more experience of the world, I think.'

'But will Sarah ever forgive me?' wondered Muriel. 'She's so furious with me.'

'She'll calm down. Sarah doesn't harbour grudges. You'll just have to have patience, Muriel.'

'I ... I've never had a child of my own,' Muriel said, still a trifle tearful. 'I've got to thinking of Sarah as my daughter, and I think I love her as much as I would have loved a child of my own.'

'I understand,' said Constance, and put a hand on her friend's arm.

Sarah heard the words, and paused, then turned towards the kitchen, her feelings again in battle against themselves. She was still furious with Aunt Muriel, but now her anger was tempered by other emotions. She could see that it was only concern for her welfare which had caused Aunt Muriel to make such a scene. She had been frightened for her, and it was her way of protecting her. With Sarah, Aunt Muriel was often far from her usual cool-headed self.

But Simon was different, she thought, her heart sore. Simon had no such excuse. He was convinced she had been responsible for all his setbacks, even if indirectly, and she would have to pay for it.

Unless she *did* find the culprit. Would the mischief stop after Clifford went? If it continued, then that in itself would clear him.

A short time later Cliff came storming in the kitchen door, and made for the stairs to his attic bedroom.

'Clifford!' cried Sarah. 'Wait! I want to talk to you.'

'Well, I've had enough of talking,' said Cliff. 'I didn't mess up the Chief's roses, but I damn well wish I had. Not that he accused me. Oh, no! he was too wily for that, but he was sure in a rage over you. We had a good shouting match.' Clifford stopped suddenly and grinned. 'He's not so bad, your old Simon. He's a fighter, anyway, and I wish him the best of luck.'

'I wanted to come with you, Cliff,' she told him. 'Only I've no money.'

'Well, I've precious little either,' he told her, 'and anyway, what good would that do? You don't love me, do you?'

She shook her head slowly.

'Not like that, though I do love you in a way, and I think you feel the same way about me. I don't suppose I'd be much help to you. Where are you going? Back to Humberton?'

He shook his head.

'No, as a matter of fact, I've got plans. I may be able to get a job ... in the neighbourhood.'

'Let me know then. Ring me up and we can meet somewhere and talk, and if things keep happening here, they'll know it wasn't you. I want to be around to tell them so.'

'Well, don't tell them too loudly, or they'll

think you cooked up the idea just to prove the point.'

'They wouldn't!'

'Oh no? Don't try it, anyway, Sarah. Boy, haven't you got an old dragon for an aunt!'

Sarah shook her head.

'No, she isn't really,' she defended. 'She's only concerned for me.'

'You could fool me,' Cliff told her.

She changed the subject.

'Have … have you said goodbye to Ruth?'

Clifford's face went hard.

'I hardly think she'll be interested or even notice me going,' he told her flatly, then bent to kiss her on the cheek. 'See you again, love,' he told her, and grinned cheekily at Simon who had come in and was watching them.

'It's O.K., boss, Ah's goin',' he said. 'Ah'll relieve this 'ere plantation of mah unwelcome presence.'

Simon glared.

'I'm going out,' he barked to Sarah. 'Tell Mother I shan't be in for any meals today. I shall probably be back late.'

Clifford turned and winked at Sarah as Simon strode past both of them and slammed the door.

'Let's hope he meets a pieman or he'll be starving. Simple Simon met a pieman, going...'

'Oh, do shut up!' cried Sarah, her nerves all on edge. 'Shut up, Cliff. I'm glad he's going out. I'm fed up with both of you, you and Simon. I'm even fed up with Bonny-grass!'

She covered her face with her hands, and Clifford again put his bony arms round her, and held her comfortingly.

'Don't upset yourself, Sarah. See, nothing's that bad. Not even jail. And here's Mrs White shuffling along the hall, so dry up, there's a good girl. Simon's done me a good turn, giving me the sack, so long as he makes it clear to everybody that it wasn't for messing about among the roses. I needed a push in the right direction, and this may be it.' He bent and kissed her again. 'I'll tell you when I'm settled. Chin up! That's my Sarah. I'll just give Mrs White a big kiss, too.'

Dinner that day was an unwholesome meal, salted by Sarah's tears, and toughened by Mrs White's rough treatment and Mrs Demaine's neglect. No one felt like doing anything, and even Ruth didn't grumble about doing some of Sarah's jobs.

As for Sarah, she had never felt more miserable in her life. Cliff was gone and Simon had put her in the doghouse. She felt annoyed with Aunt Muriel, and Mrs Demaine was giving her a wide berth. Even Mrs White was brokenhearted at seeing Clifford go.

Sarah went out to the back door for a breath of fresh air, and hardly cared when she saw Bobby Mather lurking around.

'Can I talk to you, miss?' he asked.

'What about?'

'That young student getting the blame for that rose and them other things.'

'What about them?'

'I don't think he done it.'

'Tell me something I don't know,' said Sarah tiredly.

Bobby's manner suddenly took on its usual swagger after he had assured himself that Jem was nowhere in sight.

'Is it worth a date?' he asked.

'No.'

'Oh no?'

'No. Give up, Bobby, do. Nothing's worth a date with you.'

'Not even if I know who was seen talking all cosy to that there Vause chap? Saw them meself in Kendal.'

'Who?' demanded Sarah.

'Ah. It's not worth a date, so why should I tell you?'

But Sarah's morning had been too shattering to rise to the bait.

'Why indeed?' she asked. 'Keep it to yourself, Bobby. I wouldn't even know whether or not you were telling the truth.'

'Oh, all right,' he said sulkily, and

suddenly looked like a peeved boy. 'You can't blame a man for trying.'

Sarah couldn't help giggling. Bobby was so determined to be a Romeo!

'I must go, Bobby,' she said, more kindly. 'I'm sorry, but really, I don't want to come out with you. I'm much too old for you, and I'm not your type.'

'I like older girls,' he told her earnestly. 'And anyway, you're hardly any older than me. I used to like Ruth Kirkham, but she … she…'

Bobby glowered, and Sarah stifled another laugh, imagining the treatment he'd get from Ruth!

'It was her,' he said sullenly. 'She was in one of the big hotels in Kendal with that there Raymond Vause. All close together, too. Just ask her and see.'

Bobby swung away, and Sarah leaned her back against the garden fence, hardly able to take in what Bobby was saying. That it was Ruth who was so friendly with Raymond Vause. Ruth! She didn't believe it!

Sarah walked slowly back to the house. She didn't believe it! Not Ruth. It couldn't be Ruth. Yet she couldn't help remembering Ruth's white face when Clifford was blamed. Was that because of her own guilt?

Yet why should Ruth do such a thing? She loved Bonnygrass and would never harm it. Would Raymond Vause offer her money to do such a thing?

Suddenly Sarah remembered something from the past, and it was with her as clear as yesterday. It was old Jem Johnson's telling her ... warning her? ... that Raymond Vause was too free with his money. Was that what Jem meant? Did he know something about it? Did he know that Vause was bribing someone, and if he did, he might also know who.

Sarah felt like rushing off to find Jem, but instead she walked back to the house. She had had enough for one day, and she was gradually learning patience and caution. Jem was a very cautious person, and he would have to be approached carefully.

Sarah felt she needed more time to think, in order to sort out the whole problem.

But she felt better now, as she marched into the dining room and began to help Mrs White, hearing her aunt and Mrs Demaine talking companionably in the lounge.

'I'll help wash up,' she offered, 'then I must get over to the office.'

'All right, luv,' said Mrs White mechanically, 'but I don't know what the house is coming to, that I don't. It don't seem like home no more.'

'It will again,' Sarah assured her. 'Don't worry, Mrs White. It will sort itself out, you'll see.'

CHAPTER NINE

The house took a long time to settle down after Clifford left. Simon was very morose and moody, while Ruth seemed even more unlike her usual self. Sarah felt as though the other girl was hardly able to tolerate her, and this at first upset her, then made her angry. Why should she feel guilty because of Ruth, while all the time...

She considered Ruth thoughtfully one morning, the memory of Bobby's words uppermost in her mind. So far she hadn't been able to have a word with Jem. The old man seemed to be avoiding her, and she heard Thomas remark to Simon that he was a bit under the weather these days, and could do with a few days' holiday. Sarah had left the matter of talking to him till Jem was feeling better, but often she longed to ask

Ruth about Raymond Vause. She hated harbouring suspicions about people, and preferred to have things out in the open.

Though last time, when she tackled Clifford, she hadn't made a very good job of it, and hadn't really cleared the air at all.

Matters came to a head when Ruth found that she had to arrange floral decorations for an important function the following night, and didn't know anything about it. The organisers rang up with a small adjustment, and she listened, perplexed, but took a note of the new arrangement then put down the telephone.

'I've no note of this,' she said, looking in her diary, 'yet they say they rang up about it last week.'

Sarah's brows wrinkled in thought.

'They did,' she said. 'I took that call.'

'*You* did? Then for heaven's sake why didn't you tell me? Honestly, Sarah, I don't know why Simon thinks you're becoming quite competent. You can do far more damage in here than anyone I know.'

'That's not fair!' flashed Sarah. 'I left a note on your desk, clearly written out. I don't know why you haven't seen it. As for doing damage, you're maybe a fine one to talk. Is it true you've been seeing Raymond Vause … having a meal with him in Kendal, for instance?'

Ruth went white, then flushed scarlet with rage.

'Oh!' she said. 'Oh! That's just the last straw. How dare you spy on me! You've blamed Clifford and got rid of him, even if he is … is a nice boy … far too nice for you! And now you blame me. How dare you! For your information, I *did* see Ray Vause in Kendal … on my father's behalf. He is very kindly donating a stained glass window to our church, and as secretary of the Parochial Church Council, I was asked to consult him about it. He preferred to discuss it over a meal, though why I should explain myself to you I've no idea!'

'Why indeed?' asked Simon, who had come in during the middle of the row.

'Because I had to know,' cried Sarah. 'I'm just as keen as anybody to clear up the cloud which seems to hang over everybody here. You can't blame me for exploring any possibility which will clear Cliff...'

'Well, you won't clear him by blaming me,' flashed Ruth, 'much as you'd like to. If ... if it had been me, do you think I'd have let Cliff take the blame?'

There was a hint of tears in Ruth's voice, and Sarah looked at her closely. Was she really concerned about Clifford, or was it anger at being wrongfully accused? Her own cheeks were hot, and once again she was hating herself inside. It was horrible accusing people who were innocent, and she avoided Simon's eyes in case she read contempt in them.

'I ... I'm sorry,' she said chokily. 'Someone ... someone saw you and told me.'

'Who would tell you?'

'It doesn't matter,' said Sarah.

It would do no good to turn Ruth's wrath on Bobby. The boy irritated her, but she had no wish to get him into trouble, too.

'All these accusations!' Ruth was crying. 'Maybe they're just to cover up for yourself, Sarah. Oh, I don't say you're deliberately setting out to ruin Bonnygrass, but when you think about them, they could be caused by sheer incompetence, and you've got plenty of that *You've* maybe done it all with your own stupidity.'

It was Sarah's turn to go white, and she ignored Simon's quick interruption, no doubt intended to keep the peace.

'It's not true. You can't say that when it just isn't true. And I never went near the new rose. Simon knows that. I was nowhere near it at all!'

'All right, all right, Sarah,' said Simon, putting an arm round her shoulder. 'That's enough, my dear. Look, there's no good in everybody flying off the handle and hurling accusations at each other's head. There's been no further damage done since Ainslie left, and I rather think we got the culprit when we asked him to leave. I'm sorry,

Sarah. I ... I know you cared for him a lot, and I don't think he quite realised what he was doing when he ruined the flowers. I think most of it *was* incompetence ... *his* incompetence, and he's probably sorry now, but unwilling to admit to it. He's rather a nice boy, really, but he's inclined to take things far too lightly and bob along on the surface.'

'I think he feels things much more deeply than you realise,' Sarah defended. 'Clifford has been stupid in the past, but I think he's grown up now, same's I had to do. I don't think he would ever have harmed the rose because he knew very well how long it had taken to develop it. He wouldn't destroy so many years of work.'

'Your impassioned plea is a little late now, Sarah,' said Ruth. 'If I were you, I'd shut up now. You've heard the saying "Methinks the lady doth protest too much" or similar. Well, that's what it sounds like.'

Simon, too, had the hard look back on his face.

'Nevertheless, we *have* had no further sabotage,' he said coldly. 'That's what counts as far as I'm concerned.'

'Don't tell her that,' said Ruth, 'or she'll be away rooting up the chrysanthemums just to prove you wrong.'

'You'll have to excuse me now,' said Sarah, rage boiling in her again as her eyes almost sparked off Ruth. 'Some people have arrived. I'll go and show them round, unless you're afraid I'll throw them into the lily-pond in Garden Number Four.'

She marched out, not seeing the sudden glint in Simon's eyes. Ruth didn't see it either. Her eye had fallen on a square white piece of paper clipped to her 'pending' file. Written on it, in Sarah's neat hand, were precise instructions for the floral decorations required the following day.

Ruth bit her lip. She must have looked at it quite a few times without really taking it in. She owed Sarah an apology, and knew she would have to make it. She ran a hand over her forehead, thinking she must pull herself together a bit better. She'd never neglected anything in her life before, least of all her job.

The following Monday Mrs Demaine suddenly realised that Muriel had been at Bonnygrass for almost a week and had seen nothing yet of the beautiful scenery around Kendal.

'You can come with me this afternoon,' offered Simon. 'I'm going to Grasmere. I'm sure you'll like Grasmere. It's one of my own favourite places.'

'Oh yes, Aunt Muriel, it's gorgeous,' Sarah told her.

The sharp upset of the past few days was beginning to pass now, and although Sarah felt that her normal lightness of spirit had been well damped down, she was beginning to adjust and to put it behind her. If Cliff would only telephone and say he was quite all right, and not starving for bread and butter, she would be happy to forget all about it and get on with her work. Ruth had offered her a generous apology about the phone call, which she had carefully noted, and she had been happy to apologise in return. Their row had cleared the air a little, but Sarah could feel that Ruth still resented her, and that there couldn't be real friendship between them.

It certainly couldn't be because of Simon, thought Sarah wryly. Ruth would have to be out of her mind to think of her as a possible rival for his affections. Nor could it be Clifford, since Ruth had obviously now accepted his dismissal, and didn't seem at all curious as to where he had gone. It was Sarah who worried over that.

'Can't Sarah come with us?' Aunt Muriel was asking, as she gladly accepted his offer of an outing to Grasmere.

'Oh no, Aunt Muriel,' said Sarah hastily, 'it's Monday. I have to help in the house today, and you never know when people are going to turn up.'

'Nonsense, my dear,' said Mrs Demaine firmly, 'of course we can spare you. Ruth will deal with customers and Mrs White and

I will soon see to everything in the house. You have little enough time off as it is. Hasn't she, Simon?'

'Yes, of course,' said Simon shortly, and Sarah felt hot with embarrassment. It was obvious to her that Simon didn't want her.

'I don't want to go,' she said clearly, but he brushed this aside impatiently.

'Don't be silly, Sarah. Get your coat on, too. It's chilly today, being dull. I'll load up the estate car with the things I'm taking. I've only got one call to make.'

'There you are, dear,' said Aunt Muriel delightedly. 'Go and put on that pretty yellow dress.'

Sarah couldn't argue further, though she wished people would mind their own business, and scowled at Simon through the window. He looked up, caught sight of her, and suddenly grinned. Sarah drew back, blushing, then hurried to put on the dress, her heart swelling a little. Just when she usually worked up a good anger against Simon, he'd smile at her, or hug her shoulders. It wasn't fair! She didn't really want to love him because it was no fun being in love with someone who obviously didn't return it. But Sarah brushed her hair vigorously, and put on her brightest lipstick, then marched outside to the estate car. Aunt Muriel was already installed there ... in the back seat.

'You sit in the front, Aunt Muriel,' she suggested.

'No, Sarah. I'm nervous in a car, and I read some good advice which said that nervous people should always sit in the *back* of a car.'

'But you'd see more in the front.'

'Of course I won't. I'll see just as much from the back, and you can tell me where it all is.'

'Get in,' said Simon briefly.

Sarah got in.

Simon had to drive slowly through the Lakeland towns and along the winding roads. Even on Monday they were busy with holidaymakers, and young people dressed for walking or climbing. Some of them reminded Sarah of Clifford, and she began to look more closely in case he was among them somewhere. He had said he wasn't going to leave the area.

Aunt Muriel was glad that Simon was driving with caution. Not only could she enjoy fine views of the lakes and mountains, and study the lovely small villages, but her nerves were set at rest sitting behind a good driver.

'It's all very beautiful,' she said, looking out eagerly. 'I love that lovely stone or slate they use for building the houses and walls ... even the new ones. It blends so beautifully with the landscape.'

'Yes, it is lovely,' said Sarah absently, staring at a lone figure walking ahead, then looking behind at his face when the car flashed past.

'What are you looking for, dear?' asked Aunt Muriel curiously, having seen this happen more than once.

'To see if Cliff's around,' said Sarah,

thoughtlessly, then wished she had kept quiet when this was greeted with frosty silence. A glance at Simon's face showed that he looked thundery, while Aunt Muriel sounded as though she was fighting for control.

'I thought we'd seen the last of that young man,' she said icily. 'I've no wish to have my day ruined by being reminded of him, Sarah.'

'Sorry,' said Sarah mechanically, but she only half gave up her search. Simon could glower if he liked!

A sudden shaft of sunlight lit up the dull day and Sarah was suddenly reminded of her last trip here with Simon, and her heart began to feel heavy. That had been a happy day! She glanced at Simon, wondering if he had remembered it, too, at any time. But he was merely looking grim and was driving with great concentration.

'Can we have tea in Grasmere?' asked Aunt Muriel.

There was silence for a while, then Sarah

ventured an answer.

'Simon's the one who knows all the places for tea.'

Her voice had an edge to it, and he shot a glance at her.

'Certainly we can have tea at Grasmere, Aunt Muriel,' he answered evenly. 'I always offer my girl-friends tea when I take them out.'

Aunt Muriel's laughter was suddenly welcome, and Sarah, too, began to smile.

In the pretty tea-room, however, Aunt Muriel got up and decided she needed to freshen up, leaving Sarah and Simon at the table. There was a heavy silence while they looked at each other.

'I'm sorry you've been saddled with me,' said Sarah stiffly.

'And I'm sorry you had to be bulldozed into coming,' he told her equably. 'Too bad you didn't get your eye on your precious Clifford or that might have made it worth while.'

'I ... I just want to know he's all right,'

she said shakily.

'My God, he's a man, isn't he, not a helpless child? Or do you prefer someone helpless who needs mothering, Sarah?'

'I ... I don't know what you mean.'

'Don't you?'

'That's better,' said Aunt Muriel, returning to the table. 'Now let me see. I think I'd like some nice toast, dear. Or perhaps a ham sandwich? Yes, ham rolls. That will do fine.'

'Three ham rolls,' said Simon to the waitress, 'if that's O.K. with you, Sarah.'

'Fine,' she said, though she didn't really want to eat anything at all.

On the way home, only Aunt Muriel kept up the conversation. Then she, too, lapsed into silence and sighed a little. What a pity Sarah and Simon didn't get on a little better, she thought with disappointment. There really was little to hope for in that direction. She would have liked Simon for Sarah, even if they had to be poor for a little while. She felt she could trust him, and Constance would make such a nice mother-in-law. That, decided Muriel, was very important.

Still, we can't all get what we want in this world. Life often dishes out disappointments and she'd had her share. She should be used to them by now.

The following morning Sarah learned that old Jem Johnson was ill in bed and hadn't been able to come to work. Mrs White gave her the news, having just spoken to Thomas at the back door.

'Oh dear, I do hope he isn't bad,' she said worriedly. 'I'll have to walk up to the cottage and see him. Is anyone looking after him?'

'Mrs Mather will be seeing to him, Miss Sarah, luv,' the other woman told her. 'She's a good-hearted soul.'

'Nevertheless, I'll run up and see him as soon as I can arrange it,' Sarah decided.

But it was Mrs Mather who came to fetch her about an hour later, coming round hesitantly to the back door.

'He's fretting for a word with you, Miss

Sarah,' she said apologetically. 'I hope it won't put you out of your way.'

'I'll come at once,' Sarah told her, looking worried at the stout pleasant woman who was Bobby's mother. 'What's wrong with him, Mrs Mather? Has he overtired himself like Mrs Demaine? They remind me of each other now and again. I think it's because they're so determined to do their best.'

'That's probably it, Miss Sarah. He's a bit weak and tired, and I've got the doctor coming to have a look at him. He needs a rest, most likely.'

Jem did look pale, for him, when Sarah saw him propped up in bed, but he greeted her eagerly, and asked her to sit down, and talk to him.

'She'll keep me company if you want to go home and see to your own house, Jessie,' he advised Mrs Mather.

The older woman hesitated.

'Well, if you're sure...'

'I can spare a couple of hours, Mrs Mather.'

'If you want me, I'll just be across the road, and I'll be back with a bowl of soup for you, Jem, at dinnertime.'

'You're a good lass,' he said, and suddenly looked very tired. 'Aye, she's a fine good woman,' he repeated to Sarah after Mrs Mather had gone, 'but it's because of her I've done a lot o' wrong, Miss Sarah. I did it because Jessie has been good to me, but now … now…' Jem's thorny fingers trembled as he plucked at the bed-covers. 'Now I'm tired, and I'm afraid it's me heart, so I thought I'd better tell you, in case I popped off sudden-like, then no one would know that young man got the sack for nowt.'

Sarah's eyes grew round, partly with alarm for Jem, then with surprise at his words.

'Do … do you mean Clifford Ainslie, Jem?'

'Aye, I do. He could be a cheeky young monkey at times, but he never touched rose. Nor did he turn off heaters or kill off any plants. It were that Mr Vause that were responsible, him being so free with his money.'

Sarah stared at Jem, perplexed. Surely ... surely *Jem* wouldn't do such a thing for money! Suddenly she felt far more afraid for the old man than she had ever done for Cliff. If it had been Jem then Simon would never get over it ... an old man he'd trusted for years, and his father before him...

'You ... you didn't do it, Jem, did you?' she asked, her mouth dry and her eyes large with anxiety.

'Me? Me do such a thing? Eh, I'd have to be out of me mind!'

Sarah almost laughed in her relief, not only at Jem's denial, but at the strength of it. He had just been like his usual self, and she couldn't help feeling that his present ailment was mental and not physical.

'Then who did?' she asked directly. 'If you ask me, you've put yourself in bed with worry, so get it off your chest and you'll be out of there in no time.'

'Maybe you're right, Miss Sarah, because I've been that worried, wondering what to do, knowing where me duty lay then thinking about the woman who's been so good to me. I couldn't do nowt wi' the boy either. He's full o' sauce, and he knew I wouldn't say owt because of his mother...'

'Bobby! It was Bobby!'

'Aye, the young rip, it were 'im. He were swaggering about spending more than's good for him, then I caught on to it when I saw that there Vause talking to him, and I tackled him. Paying him to make mischief for Mr Simon, he were. Wants the land, ye see. I warned young Bobby, but he knew ... he knew about his mam, ye see...'

'But surely mischief like Bobby did wouldn't be so drastic for Simon? Surely Mr Vause would know that?'

'The rose could have made money for him. It were a lovely rose his father started years ago. A bi-colour, pink and lavender. There's money in developing new roses and if you could get a black one ... well, millions most likely.'

'A black rose! How horrible!'

'Ah, you might think so, but a black rose,

now, that would be the thing. Make millions.'

Sarah was silent.

'Simon will have to be told, Jem, even … even if it does upset Mrs Mather. It was wrong of you to keep quiet. I mean, Clifford's more or less been blamed for it, maybe not in so many words, but he's lost his job just the same. Besides, Bobby could have done even more harm.'

'Not with my eye on him like it was. I put fear o' God into him after rose, though that were enough, goodness knows. That were cruellest thing he could have done, and I knew then I'd have to tell on him, though every time poor Jessie brought a pie over, or washed and ironed me curtains, I felt torn in two. Who were stronger? I wondered. Mr Simon or Jessie? It fair set me ill thinking about it.'

Sarah bit her lip.

'Have you told Mrs Mather?' she asked, and the old man shook his head.

'Like me to tell her for you?'

Again Jem shook his head.

'No, Miss Sarah, that's my job. I'll tell her first, then if you ask Mr Simon to come and see me when he can spare the time, I'll tell him, too. Only I thought I'd talk it over with you first, then I'd see clear where me duty lay.'

'You knew that already, Jem. You should have told Simon before, and he might not have lost the rose.'

'I know, lass,' said Jem miserably. 'That's why I say it were all my fault. I'm to blame. I expect I'll get sack, too.'

'That'll be up to Simon,' said Sarah, rather tiredly.

At least Clifford would be cleared, she thought, and felt relieved for his sake. She wished he would get in touch with her soon, so that she could tell him. He'd be angry no doubt, being Cliff, and would have plenty to say.

Then she thought of Simon. How upsetting it would be for him, knowing it was one of his own men who had done this, even if Bobby was young. He'd known the family for years. She should have guessed, thought Sarah, remembering how the boy had swaggered before her. Simon had said he wasn't very intelligent, and it had been short-sighted of him to do such a thing. He might have had a good future in Bonnygrass. Now, no doubt, he had spent the hand-out from Vause, and he would be out on his ear without a reference. Sarah spared a thought for his mother who didn't seem to deserve being worried like this.

But Simon hadn't deserved to lose his rose, decided Sarah. She remembered the dull look in his eyes, when he first knew about it. Simon had been hurt inside, and Sarah, remembering, knew her sympathy was all for him.

'I'll get Mrs Mather,' she told the old man. 'You'd better tell her, Jem. You'll feel tons better when it's off your mind, and you know, it's really Mrs Mather's responsibility, too. I … I guess she must have spoiled Bobby.'

'Maybe you're right,' Jem told her.

He was looking better already, with more colour in his face. Sarah was glad the doctor was giving him a check-up, but she felt sure Jem was as strong, physically, as ever he was.

'I'll come and see you again tomorrow,' she promised, and suddenly bent and kissed his cheek.

'You're a fine lass,' the old man told her huskily. 'But don't be in too big a rush over that young chap Clifford. He's a nice enough lad, but you could do better than him. If he'd been right for you, Miss Sarah, I'd never have let him be blamed!'

Sarah blinked, finding it difficult to follow Jem's logic. So Cliff was allowed to take the blame because he wasn't good enough for her!

She patted the bed-covers into place and went to find Mrs Mather, who gave her a beaming, welcoming smile.

'Eh, I'm sure you'll have done him good, luv,' she told Sarah happily. 'He needs cheering up, does old Jem.'

Sarah nodded non-committally, her eyes full of sympathy. No doubt Bobby was now out on a job with Thomas, who would want to give him a good hiding when he found out.

Sarah walked back home, and gave Simon the message.

'Is he … is he rather ill?' asked Simon carefully.

'Not physically, I don't think,' said Sarah, avoiding his eyes. 'He … he wants to talk to you.'

Simon looked at her piercingly, and Sarah avoided his eyes.

'I'll see him this afternoon,' he said decisively. 'Thank you, Sarah.'

Simon came back around five, looking like a thundercloud. He asked for Bobby Mather to be sent to him as soon as he returned, and disappeared into his office where he picked up the telephone, and asked to speak to Raymond Vause.

Then the door banged shut and Ruth

looked inquiringly at Sarah.

'What's eating Simon?'

Sarah knew very well, but she didn't feel like discussing it with Ruth. What would she say, wondered Sarah uneasily, when she knew that Clifford was completely in the clear? Sarah had never been able to guess what Ruth really felt about Clifford. He had been rather a challenge to Ruth and Sarah knew he'd gone to her Youth Club several times, which must have given the older girl quite a lot of satisfaction.

'Has anyone else been doing damage?' asked Ruth, and this Sarah was able to answer.

'No, I don't think so. Things have been rather quiet today.'

'We'll have to get more men if old Jem's going to be off very long, especially now that Clifford has gone, too.'

'And Bobby,' said Sarah thoughtlessly.

'Bobby? *He* hasn't handed in his notice, has he? Is that why Simon wants to see him?'

Sarah flushed and looked guilty. 'I ... er...'

'What's so secret that I can't be told?' asked Ruth angrily. 'I can tell by your face something's up.'

'Here's Bobby now,' said Sarah hurriedly, looking out of the window. 'Thomas has just arrived in the van.'

The interview was fairly brief, and since the door hadn't been completely closed, the girls heard every word. Simon's voice was icy with rage and for once Bobby was unable to bluster his way out of it, and took it all in silence apart from his heavy, laboured breathing which betrayed his fright.

'Only regard for your mother prevents me from having the law on you,' Simon said tightly, 'but it I ever catch you anywhere near Bonnygrass, I'll break your neck. Now get out, and don't let me set eyes on you again!'

Bobby got out quick, and Sarah, her cheeks scarlet, stole a look at Ruth as Simon walked slowly through from the office.

'I hardly think we're likely to have more

trouble now,' he said heavily, 'either from anyone inside Bonnygrass ... or outside.'

'Very nice,' said Ruth. Her cheeks, too, were scarlet and her eyes sparked with anger. 'And what about Clifford Ainslie? I suppose it doesn't matter about him?'

Simon nodded, then sat down wearily in his chair.

'I know. I'm sorry about young Ainslie, though he was never accused of being responsible, you know. I thought it best that he should go at the time. Don't you know where he is, Sarah? I'd like to...'

'Apologise,' finished Ruth. 'That, of course, will tidy everything up nicely. And why should Sarah know where he is? She hasn't been so terribly concerned for him, has she? No, if you want to know where he is, you can ask me!'

Sarah saw shock register on Simon's face as he stared at her.

'What do you mean, Ruth?'

The older girl's composure was beginning to crack.

'I was the only one who cared about him,' she told them defiantly. 'I'm the only one who knows how to handle him, too. Clifford's a very clever boy, and very talented, and if you want to know, he's got a good job now in photography. He was nearly trained when he had to leave college, and your aunt had no right to blame him for spoiling things for you, Sarah. In fact, it was you who nearly spoiled his life. *You* could have influenced him, if you'd had any guts, but no!... You let him behave stupidly and didn't bother to talk one iota of horse sense into him.

'Anyway, Daddy knew people in advertising who have taken Clifford on, and he loves it. We ... we're going to be married as soon as he's settled down and can find a flat. I ... I'll want to leave next month, Simon, because we'll be living in Manchester, and I shall get a job there. We should manage very well.' She was silent for a moment. 'I ... I was going to have told you as soon as I could, but with being short-staffed...'

There was utter silence in the office as Ruth's voice trailed off and Sarah, stealing a glance at Simon, read pain in his eyes as they met hers. Her own heart grew heavy and cold. So now he had lost Ruth to Clifford!

She bit her lip. For a while it had seemed that she had harmed Bonnygrass by being responsible for Clifford coming here, then after Jem told her the truth, she was glad that his name had been cleared, for her own sake as well as his.

But now she had spoiled Simon's happiness in a completely different way. Because if Clifford hadn't come here, he would never have met Ruth and … and … Sarah forced back the tears … lost her for Simon. Because it was easy to see that this had been a blow to him, and perhaps the biggest one of all.

'I … I'm sorry, Simon,' Ruth was saying. 'Could I go now? I … I want to see Clifford and tell him the good news. He's still in Kendal and staying with friends of ours, before going to Manchester. I … I think he ought to know as soon as possible.'

'Yes, of course,' said Simon, rather hoarsely. 'Go now, Ruth, if you want.'

'I'm sorry I had to tell you like this,' she said, lifting down her coat. 'I'll see you aren't stuck as far as work is concerned. I'll soon find you the right person to take my place.'

He waved a hand to indicate that it didn't matter, and Sarah began to feel angry. How dared Ruth keep hurting him like this, as though completely unaware of his feelings! She was selfish, thought Sarah, completely selfish, sorting out her own affairs and talking about it so glibly to Simon who had just been dealt another body blow. So far she had been silent, but now she glared at Ruth.

'I hope you'll be very happy,' she said, her voice jagged with anger.

Ruth paused, then smiled sweetly.

'Why, thank you, Sarah. I'll pass on your message to Clifford. Goodnight, both of you.'

She swept out, leaving both of them in complete silence. Sarah felt the tears welling up and tried to force them down. But it had been an upsetting day, and she couldn't control them.

She felt Simon's arms round her, comfortingly.

'Oh, Simon, I'm so sorry,' she told him huskily. 'I … I seem to have made an awful mess of things, bringing Clifford here.'

'You certainly have. You don't seem very good at handling things, do you?'

'No.'

She wept for a few moments.

'I'm sorry.'

'So am I,' he told her gruffly. 'Come on, let's go into the house. I'll get Mother and Aunt Muriel to pour some hot tea down you. As for me … well, I need something a bit stronger!'

Sarah didn't doubt it.

CHAPTER TEN

Aunt Muriel went home on Saturday. She had had a good holiday, and it had been very pleasant having Constance to talk to, and to remember the happy days of their youth now that the unhappy days were completely forgotten.

The holiday had done them both good. Mrs. Demaine was more satisfied than ever with Bonnygrass, thinking there was a lot to be said for having a nice spacious house which was satisfying to manage, and plenty of people around to keep her happy. She didn't envy Muriel being on her own in a flat.

On the other hand, Muriel was looking forward to life in the flat again. She loved the challenge of her career, and would hate to stagnate as a housewife, she decided.

Bonnygrass was charming, but it must be an awful headache to Constance, and really, there was nowhere you could get any real peace with people clumping out and in all the time.

Besides, she might soon have Sarah back with her again … and this time without that young Clifford trailing behind! Fancy that sensible girl Ruth wanting to marry him and her father, a vicar, giving his consent. Muriel wondered what the parishioners thought when they saw Clifford in their midst.

Ah well, there was no accounting for taste, she thought, with a sigh. She would have expected Sarah and Simon, now, to fall into each other's arms, but no such luck. She would even have been encouraged if they'd fought a little and started hating each other. But they did none of these things, and seemed anxiously polite to one another, which Muriel found rather depressing. She hadn't been short of boy-friends in her day, and although she had never married, she had been wooed ardently by more than one young man.

In those days, she decided, young men had far more charm and energy. In fact, she wouldn't be surprised if that young Ruth hadn't proposed to Clifford, instead of the other way round.

Sarah came in to say goodbye to her aunt.

'I've been thinking over what you said, Aunt Muriel,' she said, rather hesitantly, 'about a career, I mean. I … I think I'd like to train for a career of some kind. Maybe I could get in somewhere as a trainee designer, and take typing and shorthand at night classes. I was wondering if you could look into it for me for September.'

'But of course, darling. If that's what you want.'

It wasn't what Sarah wanted, but it looked like being what Sarah was going to get. She was becoming rather fed up at Bonnygrass. Simon had now decided to be kind to her, treating her very gently and leaning over backwards to keep his temper if she did anything wrong. Sarah would much rather he'd thrown the ink at her. She had even thrown a tantrum herself, but he had only treated it with heavy sympathy and understanding.

He had been lucky enough to find a good workman who had been a gardener to old Colonel Vause, and Jem Johnson had recovered in a surprisingly short time. Mrs Mather seemed to have dealt very firmly with Bobby, who announced to everyone that he was fed up with this backwater and was going to join the Army.

'That'll fix him,' Jem said, with satisfaction. 'Let him try his tricks in the Army, and see how far it gets him. He'll have sergeant to reckon with, and he won't pat him on the head like his mum used to do. Oh no!'

The departure of Bobby had put new life into Jem, and now the wheels were rolling again at Bonnygrass, as Thomas and Owen Weekes got used to each other's ways, and began to work companionably together.

Ruth had also found them a good secretary. Hilda Naylor was a widow, in her early forties, with a grown-up son in the Civil Service. Her typing and shorthand had been a little rusty at first, but she was quietly competent, and both Sarah and Simon liked her a great deal. They had both been invited to Ruth's wedding, and Sarah bit her lip when Simon came to look for her.

'You want to go, Sarah?' he asked. 'You needn't, if you don't want, but...'

He paused, and she knew what he was asking her to do. He himself would be obliged to go, and it might be quite a lot easier if he had Sarah by his side. It couldn't be much fun for him seeing Ruth married off to someone else.

'Of course I'll go,' she told him, and lifted her chin proudly. 'I'm already planning something nice to wear. We mustn't let Bonnygrass down.'

'That's my girl, Sarah,' he said softly, and a sudden memory came to her of Clifford saying those very words. Her eyes sobered and she felt very glad he was going to be happy, even if he had pinched Simon's girl.

'Penny for them,' said Simon, watching her expressive face.

'Oh, nothing. I was just remembering...'

Sarah broke off and the smile left Simon's face. For a moment he looked furious, and Sarah drew back a little. Then Simon controlled himself with an effort.

'Just what has Ainslie got that I haven't?' he asked wryly, though Sarah could sense the anger still in him. 'Long hair? Sideburns? Pink shirts? I must try them all some time.'

'No, don't!' she said impulsively. 'It ... it wouldn't suit you.'

He considered her thoughtfully.

'No, I don't suppose it would.' He picked up one of her pretty pink boxes with 'Bonnygrass Bouquets' written across it in gold. It had been packed with dainty flowers for Aunt Muriel and now he handed it to her, saying he'd get out the estate car and drive Aunt Muriel to the station.

'She'll love this,' said Sarah, looking at the box.

'That was a good idea of yours, Sarah. They sold very well, so I've ordered quite a lot more.'

Sarah flushed at the praise.

'My designing wasn't too bad, then,' she said lightly. 'I might make a name for myself yet, if I go back to it.'

'Is that what you want to do?'

'I'm thinking it over,' she said evasively. 'It would make a good career.'

'Yes,' said Simon heavily.

Now she handed the box to Aunt Muriel and kissed her fondly. The older woman didn't want her to come to the station.

'I'll be seeing you soon, anyway, Sarah,' she said as she snapped her case shut, then looked at her lovely box. 'Oh, isn't it pretty!'

'I designed the box,' said Sarah proudly.

'Then I must keep it,' said Aunt Muriel. 'It may come in very handy when I'm making enquiries on your behalf. Goodbye then,

Sarah darling. See you soon. I'll just say goodbye to Constance.'

The next few days were very quiet, then things began to change. Simon had decided not to exhibit at the Southport Flower Show. The events of the past few weeks had been upsetting and he felt that little could be gained by exhibiting as things stood at the moment.

However, he felt that he would still like to attend the Flower Show and asked Sarah if she would like to go along.

'You'd enjoy it,' he told her. 'Some growers manage to produce incredibly beautiful flowers in whatever field they specialise…'

'Like you might have done with Constance Demaine?'

'Like I might have done with Constance Demaine,' he agreed, rather bitterly.

He tried not to dwell on the years which had been torn away so lightly, or the itch to strangle Bobby Mather and Raymond Vause became acute, and rage would boil up in him. With an effort he turned again to Sarah.

'A day out would do us both good, and Mother doesn't want to come this year. She says she'd find it too tiring.'

'Then I'd like to come, Simon.'

'We'll go on Saturday, then,' decided Simon. 'Be ready to leave early, won't you? We like to make a day of it, you know.'

Sarah found herself looking forward to Saturday with pleasurable excitement, and planned carefully what she was going to wear. How wonderful it would be if only the shadow of Ruth didn't lie between them. If Ruth meant nothing to Simon, how lovely it would be to have a whole day off to spend like this.

In the end the weather governed her choice of clothing and as it was a fine day, she wore her pretty white suit which made her skin look like a magnolia and her hair shine almost blue-black. She knew she looked her best, and her morale got a boost when Mrs Demaine looked at her with pleasure.

'How pretty you look, Sarah,' she said admiringly. 'When I see young people dressed up these days, I often regret my age. I'm sure we didn't have half so many attractive materials available to us.'

'I still like pure new wool, silk and linen,' said Sarah. 'They're hard to beat.'

'Yes, I suppose you're right, dear. Ah, here's Simon now. Have a nice day, both of you, and I'm sure you'll enjoy it.'

Simon nodded and ushered Sarah towards the estate car without giving her a second glance. Sarah felt rather put out and the sun seemed to shine less brightly, but Simon slid into the driving seat without a word, and they headed south towards Preston.

Sarah had never been to a Flower Show before, and she was charmed with the whole exhibition. Simon's eyes were mainly for new machinery and tools, but Sarah revelled in the beautiful flowers, incredibly perfect, and the delicate perfume of the blooms was as heady as the best wine.

'It's all exquisite,' she said to Simon, her

eyes shining as she looked at the colourful display, 'but I'm sure you could do just as well, Simon … as a grower, I mean.'

For the first time he laughed with carefree amusement.

'How loyal you are, Sarah!'

'No, I mean it. These are wonderful, but I've seen flowers at Bonnygrass just as wonderful. Let's exhibit next year…'

She broke off, biting her tongue. What would it matter to her if they exhibited next year? She wouldn't be around to see it.

Luckily Simon had caught sight of some beautiful begonias which held his interest, and didn't notice her slip of the tongue.

Simon had already booked for lunch and Sarah enjoyed the meal, having worked up an appetite. She was charmed with Southport, the attractive seaside town being new to her, and Simon seemed to throw off his worries as he escorted her around and listened, indulgently, to her frank appreciation of everything.

It was quite late when they moved into the

stream of traffic towards Preston, and both were very quiet as Simon concentrated on his driving.

'It's been a lovely day,' Sarah said at length.

It had. She was grateful for it, and knew that she would treasure the memory of it long after she had left Bonnygrass and gone back to stay with Aunt Muriel.

She would miss it all so much, she thought unhappily. She had got used to the busy life, the people who came and went, the beauty of the gardens and greenhouses, and the friends she had made.

She would miss Jem and Mrs White, and the warm cosiness of Mrs Demaine whom she now loved devotedly. But most of all she would miss Simon.

She looked at the long grey road snaking ahead in the twilight, and the queerly-shaped trees which lined the road, and reached over them protectively. She could still smell the delicacy of the flowers and knew that every time she saw a beautiful rose or a carnation, or even smelled the heady perfume of wet lilacs, then her heart would be torn back to Bonnygrass, and all it meant to her.

Sarah tried to smooth down the sudden tight lump in her throat, and saw Simon steal a sudden glance at her, hoping he wouldn't notice the wetness on her eyelashes, and feeling ashamed of those tears. If he had asked her what was wrong, she would be unable to tell him, but Simon didn't ask. He merely drove on steadily, then bumped along through the gates at Bonnygrass and on up to the garage doors, then sat still for a moment.

'Shall I open them?' asked Sarah, fairly steadily, but he didn't reply.

Then suddenly he turned to her, and took her quickly into his arms, kissing her fiercely.

Sarah struggled, feeling that there was no love or gentleness in his kiss. It was as though she was being punished for what Ruth had done to him. But Simon held her all the more fiercely and she could feel the pain of his fingers gripping her shoulders.

'No, Simon no!' she gasped. 'Let go! *You* must know I ... I'd never settle for second best.'

Simon let her go abruptly, and she could feel the rage in his indrawn breath.

'Second best!' he echoed. 'My God ... second best! Is that what it is? No, Sarah, I'm quite sure that second best is no good to anyone. Get out, then, and I'll put the car away.'

'I ... I...'

She didn't want to go like this, seeing all his anger and frustration enveloping him again. After such a lovely day, too. She wanted to tell him so, but she couldn't find the words.

'It's been a lovely day. Th ... thank you.'

'You sound like a little girl at the party, being mindful of Mummy's instructions. Polite little Sarah. Thank you, Simon, for inviting me, and the jellies and ice-cream were good, too.'

She was staring at him, her eyes shining with tears which glittered in the half light.

'Go on,' he said roughly, 'party's over now. Get moving.'

'Does it hurt you so much, Simon?' she asked, her heart heavy.

'Why should that concern you,' he asked, 'whether I'm hurt or not? Why should you worry? Come to that, I haven't seen you throwing your hat in the air.'

She shook her head.

'I can't help it if I fell in love with you,' she said, too tired to care that her devastating honesty was at work again. 'I can't help it if you loved Ruth instead of me, but you shouldn't just want me because you can't have Ruth.'

Simon was suddenly as still as night, then he drew her again into his arms.

'I don't understand this, darling,' he told her, his voice soft against her hair, 'but I don't want to. I only heard you say you love me, and that's good enough for me. I thought you would never learn to care for me.'

Sarah felt she didn't understand it either, but Simon was kissing her, properly this time, and that was good enough for her, too.

'You … you mean you really do … care for me?' she asked, when she had a breath.

'Of course I love you, darling Sarah. You must surely know that by now.'

She hadn't, but somehow it didn't seem to matter any more. Her life had been winding round in circles and twisting in and out.

'Just like the monkey puzzle,' she said, against Simon's ear.

He didn't understand that either. But for the next half hour it didn't matter in the very least.

The publishers hope that this book has given you enjoyable reading. Large Print Books are especially designed to be as easy to see and hold as possible. If you wish a complete list of our books please ask at your local library or write directly to:

Dales Large Print Books
Magna House, Long Preston,
Skipton, North Yorkshire.
BD23 4ND

This Large Print Book for the partially sighted, who cannot read normal print, is published under the auspices of
THE ULVERSCROFT FOUNDATION

Other DALES Titles
In Large Print

JANIE BOLITHO
Wound For Wound

BEN BRIDGES
Gunsmoke Is Grey

PETER CHAMBERS
A Miniature Murder Mystery

CHRISTOPHER CORAM
Murder Beneath The Trees

SONIA DEANE
The Affair Of Doctor Rutland

GILLIAN LINSCOTT
Crown Witness

PHILIP McCUTCHAN
The Bright Red Business